"Blake Butler, mastermind and visionary, has sn[...] novel. What stumbles awake in the aftermath is feral and awesome in its p[...] fairy tale of an ordinary family subjected to the strange, lonesome agony known as daily life. There Is No Year is a merciless novel cleansed of joy, pumped full of fear and awe."
—Ben Marcus

"If there's a more thoroughly brilliant and exciting new writer than Blake Butler, . . . well, there just isn't. I've literally lost sleep imagining the fallout when There Is No Year drops and American fiction shifts its axis."
—Dennis Cooper

"Blake Butler is a daring invigorator of the literary sentence."
—Gary Lutz

PRAISE FOR *NOTHING*
"The klieg-light intensity of Butler's writing intimates that there is something fundamentally terrifying about what each of us does every single night, which is to pitch our minds and bodies into oblivion."
—Time

"The primary effect of sentences like these is a powerful immersion. Reading them, we are running "Blake Butler" as a kind of executable software program in the hardware of our heads."
—New York Times Book Review

"Think David Lynch. In the waking dreamscape where Butler's thoughts spin out of control, he could be De Quincy's opium-eater wandering through a Dali painting by way of a poem by Antonin Artaud."
—Atlanta Journal & Constitution

"…a disorienting, fractal-edged portal into [Butler's] increasingly elastic perception of consciousness, space-time, and metabolism."
—The Onion A/V Club

"There are some cues from the sprawling internal monologues of Nicholson Baker and the genre-defying non-fiction of William T. Vollmann in this expansive

exploration of sleeplessness, but Butler is a writer unto himself. Simply put, you haven't ever read a book like *Nothing* before. It'll keep you up at night"
—Creative Loafing Atlanta

"Lyrical…A weird, waking-dream of a memoir superbly illustrating the relentless inner spin of the insomniac."
— Kirkus

PRAISE FOR *THERE IS NO YEAR*
"[There Is No Year] is a thing of such strange beauty that digging for answers of your own will yield the rewards that only well-made art can provide."
—New York Times Book Review

"There is no novel like Blake Butler's There Is No Year. . . . Unexpectedly riveting, totally original, and frequently funny."
—Denver Post

"Calling Blake Butler's There Is No Year a novel is akin to calling René Magritte's The Treachery of Images a pipe; both works subtly expand the framework of their respective disciplines by challenging an audience that has solidified its expectations after centuries of familiarity and repetition."
—Time Out New York

"Dystopian and sinister."
—Nylon

"An endlessly surprising, funny, and subversive writer."
—Publishers Weekly

"A smoke signal on the horizon of the American literary landscape. . . . [As] if Gertrude Stein wrote the script for a Kenneth Anger film set inside of a Norman Rockwell painting to be produced for YouTube with a John Cage soundtrack. . . . [Butler's prose offers] ecstatic pleasures. . . . it bursts and cracks with inventions and constructions."
—Creative Loafing

"This artfully crafted, stunning piece of nontraditional literature is recommended for contemporary literature fans looking for something out of the ordinary. Recommended for students of literature, psychology, and philosophy, as the distinctive writing style and creative insight into the minds of one family deserve analysis."
—Library Journal

SKY SAW

Tyrant Books
676A 9th Ave. #153
New York, New York 10036
www.nytyrantbooks.com

ISBN 13: 978-0-9850235-0-8

Cover and book design by Adam Robinson
Cover illustration by Truett Dietz

SKY SAW

BLK BTLR

Tyrant Books
New York City 2012

For GianCarlo

I will pray
I will pray
I will go down low
And I will pray to you
Down as low as I can go
I will go there
And I will pray to you

– Michael Gira, "Sex, God, Sex"

Now

White cone descended in sound blister

There were the people having skin removed: to make the hood over our last evening

Cone, White cone, colored destroyed, slipped between the wall air and the bodice of the sacrificial mothers making money from the rummage of their wombs, unto the cone

Our homes turned on their sides, the sound of the descent fixed with the ripping split the image of our vision into ten and ten again, we watched the fluelight strobe from softer planets in the vision of the fly, our begging formed a prayer

The cue meat of our perfect flayed-red bodies had been for hours there arranged, stood up on gray dots in White silence for the cone, we called it god, we called our bleating mothers named into the fold of needless seeing, this could have ended where it began, could have spared the retch of splitting selves, where the anger of the firmament released a golding dew

In the patterns of the people I could see the homes bumping through the frame of dirt rising magnetized to match the cone, the other color was a skin box inscribed with the numbers of our names, and someone begging inside the begging to be released from infinite fits, as this could yes go on forever and this would yes go on, numbers remained, sod remained fit to our cerebrums where we touched inside the fold, becoming only ever one mass body, the blubber of metal lungs and unending crystal squeal

Under the sever of the folds of each skin there were mirrors being turned up toward the gold, to fix the light back at itself and in beam of it the air began to mold white and formed with cones along the bristle, there were corridors there eaten into nothing, there were the blind becoming tongues, crumpled hard under a coarse hold where no one wanted and the sandwiches were worm, the fire leading backwards into long globes where the holes would let you fall forever among dough, the cribbing of the muscles, the asking of the child, how to as well exit this wrecked body before it hits the ground under the ground, and under that, the chew

Now our unraveling for evenings and the columns of the replicating bell, a cord of child milk rising in pink glisten for the city lamp and making every person see themselves before themselves with tubes removed, the index of the body bopped with big sheaths of silver foiling, catching words where there were words, though there were very few, the colds came rolling, cinder burst in spume, chocolate winter, no condition, a bottle of the night, the words went on and on repeating in no hours crammed between, the crust eroding on the clocks, rams the size of nowhere folding through the granule of the teeth, where anyone had been bitten for any year at all, I did not know what to say, I did not know what to say or could be needed, the hammer of the grunt, pig babies falling out of holes surrounding, wired, what I needed was this flesh

No, what I'd needed was not anything about a body, it was a small leak over the house, where all these animals were writhing and making little purple pockets from their sweat, by which hand over hand for hours one might climb into a blue mark that had corroded just across the gray, the mink of all the skies folded to one sky again quilted in the money of our night, a face just behind it, I heard seething, with its flabby lips and neon teeth, speaking into our white cylindrical air with all the language to be given back to zip, back to the mime behind the moon's boob squirting ugly milk all in this life, and still no one here would stop me from Become, no one could gather at my knees, the gnats having strengthened all such bulbs around us that the speaking even would not fit, and nothing left and wives dividing, and the money in my snatch, for every hour of the day a bed bloated stone-sized on the face of waters that had risen over all old glow, all the powerwires farting bloating pellets

There must be a limit to this wall, there must be someone growing larger just beneath the growing larger that could fuck the force back toward a stall, this was *the idea we were healing under in a lexicon of domes, not a sound now even ever but something running back and forth between two nodes, and peeling upward anything that wanted near it, the mothers' laughing rendered paste, the oars of something harder than a houseface leaning down toward the soil and blistering within it something reticulated and caterpillared and so croned it could not speak, the piddle of the image wavering from great heat and spittle rising off my back, my ingrate body, my pustule system, there was no one I would not have ever left, there were so many sore beds I had turned from or fell down through and would never blink again, would never eat again, would never, and I did this every day, for every hour I was alive I ratted someone out and so did John, Mary, Mom, and so on, all the prior unnumbered names, all the flux stops and the white ones, creaming underneath, the rise of corn where that bunch hit it and something warbling for bust, to be hit hard in the center of its legendary face, the creams and rouge of Endlesswanting amassing on our arms a finer glue*

And still I could not stand beside you in the color of the cone, for each inch of me that wanted and would be cleaning there was ten feet of me that stunk, each rung of each of these connected more rungs in a cribbage system I could by no length of me infer, I did not have the body, no mind, nothing left on which to brand, suddenly I was wearing all these bracelets and these groancrowns and I was looking down upon the earth, the legions of pixel bodies screaming underneath me and raising with their hands, the curdlife in their eyes forming diagonals that split each into new soil, blood encrusted, cowing, bigger babies squirming in their tendons to get out of their whole heads and making war from underneath, bruises formed in trombone to regale me with acid squench, and yet, there at the same time, up above me, I was looking on into the butt of any other one, my arms raised in the same way up above my head and beeping with the babies also in my own folds there again, and the lather pouring from my bodice and the keyholes of my spine, and for every lick of shoulder I had there there were ten others with the same whorl, all of us looking up and onward into one, whereby, in the split, I was the godhead and the altar and the putty and the butt, I was no one for anybody and the whole air and the figurefather and the wretch, and all of this was fine still and all of this would soon I knew begin again

It did not begin again, I waited, I said the word, I fucked the Cone, I let the Cone fuck hard into my hole, I waited, it did not begin again, I said the word again, I fucked the Cone harder, I squirted come into a sound, something wriggled through my system eating all need and the need made meat in me again, and yet the hour went on lurking and still would not again begin again, I waited, I said the word, I let the Cone have all my breast, I gave my cunt my comb my belly my cerebrum my disguise, no word, I gave my ass my hair my money gave the center of my light and all their coil, gave up the years I had recovered in my pillage and what glue where I soon expected life again, gave all of that to that above me and at the same time rained it down, a liquid system of my spoiling rendered overhead coming down on the clean soil, I waited more and fucked the Cone more and fucked the Cone's friends and its clime, I rolled into it and gave over the numbers I had been keeping for better night, to index in and sit with all these hours, I gave it this and this again, I let it eat its dinner in my tonsils, I let it sell me to the digit, gave my last religion to its mother in the dark, could not stop coughing, wore the gown, split the crown in ten and ate that, shat it out, gave this to there, the Cone, the Whitened cone of Now, my lord, it would not listen, it did not begin again, it had no eyes inside it even with my body bent and taking all this passion up the ass, all this spooling in me where once I had meant to be a seamstress and now was nothing more than stone

You could ask again, you could keep going, there were two dimensions and no walk, there were the seven dens split into heavens each and someone presiding over all, a glove eye at the center of Now, it said its name and was the name forever and would spin down under dirt and eat the cord out of the dirt if this was wanted and would return and be a floor or be a cut orange on some white table seated around by many hooded men in masks, one of them a woman with a shaved head, though she would not be found, and burned on each one's left nipple one new number that had been unindexed from the charts, a glass of milk in one hand, hammer other, how to remember how to begin, how to call the number of my name into the phone that has been baking since the minute of the lock, where you were born a second child beside yourself into this white cone and the cone again, the mother of you bathing in the sludge you'd shit out of you inside a night, upon a bed called before another frame you'd meant to love and could not see, could not call by the right name in the light there with the screens descending every second made of ash, blistering the second soft between you and obliterating and descending every second there again, it did not matter that the sky had lurched down all this give already and within that some kind of sponge, a new shirt to put on and walk around in, cloud speech, this would not be yours, this would not be hours to have given back into you no matter which way inside the folding you would try, where in a warm flat room you laid down and were someone and in other ways you'd just begun, in the same ways you'd been folded upright in a white cord for the hours colded in the floor, and in the same ways you were nothing left regardless and would never sin again, would never lick again or say a number or be a body of the Crash of Now, the tone unspooling from its tip ten ways and ten again

What not yet above could not be crushed, this was the fifteenth iteration and would replicate beyond, though this still not be any new beginning and when it ended it would not end, the houses laced with blue night risen in the toning of the crystalmind, a corridor of small flags each pyramidal and seated with a center made of cream, each hiding where inside them another instance of this lock, the speaking humming through the speakerbodies magicked and lumped with lanterns down the longest corridors, the Cone's, the Cone curled queuing flues of more natural numbers with each one a little flay, guns pirouetting in the cinder, honey for a clasp, inside the bark I tried to stand up and look what fell out but all this paste I can not eat, this translucent shit of coming skin, or a person rendered from dismissal, what I gurgled, where you've been, the scorched recorder on the bedside table I would from my mind to mattress groan a blow, notes for nothing, no words, you feet beside my pillow squirting bread, somewhere down a long a long curve way beneath us a crying chowder we carried in our lungs throughout the maze of days and frottage dying in the drawers surrounding hours we could not sleep, the hole the sink makes in a person, the diagrams of chalk, let me have you, again, no prismatics, let me have you of your brine, let me let the Cone inside us and fold nothing and be nothing and what worship of the rise, worms not threads but pleasure showers, the hole I have for you alone, the walls collapsing in the headnod faction where the mirrorarmies ask us to refrain from being flesh and spittle, I put my head against you in the shower, there is a number, a kind of dynasty undid, something writhing underneath the lather, your name imprinted, your chestparts affixed in the acid of the lawn we do not have, the asphalt prison of white hours walking between engines, someone halving you from inside that machine, the blue machine I almost killed by dying, the words you could not count, glass emission, night of no breech, caught your head against the blurt, and in the white the White Cone again rises, again the pearling rounding down, where I walk into the no yard where no door is and see the stone cut into the next instance in relief, another number will be coming and yet will not appear, speak me your age, add into the silent number that one and throw the system, guide

The shrieking sound came through the ceiling. Person 1180 felt her skin go limp. Fat powder fell around her on the blond wood—powder of bodies, burst into the air from somewhere else, their hair and syllables all knitted up in the meat of what she inhaled, and in the linings of her thinking. Beyond the house, she heard the fry of insect legs in time, long needles wanting at her flesh. All the light was full of perforation.

Person 1180 had the child spread on the table. His newborn eyes sometimes changed color. They would be dark green like the father's, then next blink they matched the wall. Sometimes the whites went checkerboard or spiraled—sometimes the pupils were not there. Person 2030 had come out twenty pounds. Person 1180 had a limp she blamed on jogging and a scar she blamed on God.

The shrieking warbled at the window. The glass bent but did not break. The child began to leak black liquid as his ass raised off the table.

The tone had been appearing on the air for weeks. Its tone contained all possible timbre: every sentence ever crammed into each blink. Sometimes the tone would last for several hours, sealing the air against all other motion. It always hurt. It made Person 1180's blood go numb. It made the books fall off the bookshelves and land opened to certain pages, though when she tried to look the words would melt or disappear. No one could say what made the tone or where it came from. Tax dollars were purportedly at work.

In the yard the trees were shaking. Dirt had filled in over our glow.

The tone peeled at the nursery walls. In strips the paint flapped at 1180's head. She felt her kneecaps swelling, weighing her downward. She felt another presence in her, like the child, though longer than it, thicker than it. She touched the shaking boy there on the lacquer. Their skins became at once adhered between them. The mother could not get her hand back. The skins were smoking. The child's spine showed through his chest. 1180 yanked and yanked.

Was the child laughing at the mother?

In the pockets between shrieking, Person 1180 read aloud. She read the book she'd found wedged among the folds of the long curtain in the hall just after Person 811 left, a date whose definition she could no longer remember, nor did she know why they'd chose to hang the curtain there— the only thing it hid was flat white wall, marred with no windows. The book was the same size of the book that you hold now. The front page had an inscription handwritten to Person 1180 by someone with an illegible signature, in bright blue ink that stung her eyes:

READ THE CHILD THIS BOOK OR HE WILL SUFFER

The text on all the other pages had been printed in a code, or in a strange language she did not recognize—babbly syllables and glyph fonts, planar symbols and number reams—and yet when 1180 passed her eyes over the lines and let her voice go, she felt the syntax easing out. Her reading voice was low and burnt and came up from her linings, something old and rhythmic as it passed. Doing the speaking in this manner juggled color in her lungs and made her woozy, a kind of crystal glass around her face. Whole hours or even days might pass before she noticed she'd been suspended in that method for so long, often even in reading a single line. She did not like this feeling but could not seem to stop it. She'd thrown the book into the flood yards behind the house more times than she could count—she'd buried it, burnt it, sold it, ate it, locked it in a metal cube—and each time the book had appeared again clenched in her arms while she was sleeping. At night the night was loud and seized with lice and there was nothing else to be. Often the lingering feeling of what she'd last read made her want to take actions unimagined, things she knew she did not really want to do and never should, and so for the most part she did not do them, though some nights it was so cold.

After each page, before turning, Person 1180 would lift and hold the book up at the child so he could see it and together they would stare. The text contained no pictures beyond the way the paragraphs all seemed to congregate and blur among each other, rising colors. The child would coo and gosh and try to touch the paper. When she'd not allow him, he would shriek—a splattering mess of voice so loud it traced her brain. And yet she read, and the more she read the more he wanted, and the silence in her ribs. She could feel the hours passing between them in those moments, slapped like batter, and she could not blink or turn away until allowed.

Around the house outside the men arrived. There were very many men.

The men were nude, their thumbs were missing; they had lesions on their eyes. In the lesions were further lesions uncountably compiled, and the chalky mouth-washed blood that ran between them thrumming at the seams of where they were, soldered into cricking plastic tubes around their bodies—from when, years back, the city had mandated all one blood among ex-felons—*these men must share and wear their plasma.* Within the rancid blood, the grit amassed: grit of terror and of sad breath, swell and recession, an aging blackness in their pits—of the sky's continued creasing, of hyper-need—grit of want of spaces between buildings being filled—our silent scrying old forever.

Some of the men had cysts grown on their backs or forehead larger than the men themselves. Some had paid to have these cysts removed while others shanked them off with lengths of wire or by lying down in streets where starving dogs would chew straight through the gristle, wetting earth up with their blood. The men's newest wounds were open and incandescent and in spots spotty with attempted healing—skin that could not quite find the width to fit together, and so in the light would spit and blush.

These men were alive and always had been and always would. Once they'd had made a workforce, an army, navy. They'd bought and sold on an open market such fine goods, and each alone they'd managed small houses of their own, and wives and sons and celebrations, occasional ideas. They were men as well as women. They wanted out of where they'd been and into something they could hold. They surrounded every home, and where every home now stood no longer, a long low cold held on the world.

The men could smell the mother—her liquid, gallons, warm wet she'd hid inside her all those nights—they could feel her flesh meet on their teeth. Person 1180 had sewn herself shut once for several drier days, but the men had fixed that.

The men had hair grown in their eyes—hair the same color all over their bodies and in their stomachs, in their brains—hair that before them had lined their fathers and those men's fathers. Many of the men as well had tattoos of every word they still could think, which obscured certain portions of the men's bodies into patches of craggy, mottled ink.

The men came into Person 1180's home. They slit the windows with their tongues and knives of screaming. They pried up the vinyl siding where wreaths of spore had lodged for blossom and they wormed their way between the blue. Certain men slid their fingernails into the locks, shaped for this instant. There were so many ways of entrance and only one clear way back out.

In the front room of the house there was a picture of the house.

Through the front door window in the photo you could see the same photo behind the glass, and if you looked very close you might see the photo lodged in that photo, and in that one, though beyond that who could say what for what or why.

It was a very, very old house, and an even older picture.

Person 1180 watched the baby on the table rasping and gabbing at itself. She measured the stutter of the indention in the child's cranium, which by now should have sealed. In the slick inch-width porthole for the child's skull, 1180 sometimes saw things crawl in or out. Sometimes she'd put her eye to the knot and peer in. She saw nothing. She'd been squirted in the face. She kissed the hole and she wished into it. The children was growing faster than he should be, she thought: *this other little man.* She should not be able to distinguish hour to hour how he'd changed, the shape of his infancy already leaving his skin behind for other colors.

The mother had a resume of rancid husbands since her husband's exit, a list she kept lodged in her chest, each one that much ouched over the other, aching one another out inside the nights of screeching and endless bleeding, burned from white to orange to red to brown to black to gold inside her mind. She could not recall any of these men's numbers, nor the specific texture of their hands, though they were in her, all compounded and compounding. Each day the list grew longer one by one or two or ten. Each one she'd shown a new part of herself that they could take away and keep and keep inside them, or perhaps hang upon some wall, or maybe eat or smudge or overpower, somehow rip unto destroyed.

The child, not yet a man himself, seemed somehow smearing in the absence of the father. His waking flesh was mostly gray. His thumbprints had the grain of gravel and against certain kinds of wood would give off sparks. The last time the mother had weighed the child the scale displayed all numerals she could not read.

The child's veins would sometimes bloat and stiffen. He already had acquired all his teeth, more teeth than he should ever have at all, together. Every morning 1180 shaved a brand new mustache off her child's top lip with the electric razor the father had left behind. He had taken the straight-edged other with him, perhaps a weapon—as well, he'd taken his legs and arms that 1180 had used to calm herself and spread herself and remember at all she was there, though he'd left the locking necklace he'd given her with her photo pasted inside. Sometimes now she would open up the necklace and see not herself but blackened paper, sometimes a tiny wedge of mirror, a scratch n sniff of stew.

Most evenings now 1180 slept with the child beside her in the night, along with the child's dolls and caps and all his clothes, each of which she'd fashioned from the crap that fell into the house among its yawnings, junk blown from the remains of other houses and small polished portions of the sky—this way gathered all together there'd be sufficient mass upon the bed to bruise in the mother an illusion as if there were still someone there beside.

Someone *is* there, she would say aloud inside herself repeating. This child. My child. My son. Person two-thou-sand-and-thir-ty, my nearest number.

The mother felt the creaming liquid in her whorl.

The men were coming up the stairs. The men were chanting.

The men were made of meat.

These were the decomposing years. There was air that made the moon go blue.

These were days of no new healing, days undone by knives.

1. SAFETY SCISSORS—First known to have turned on the students in a fourth grade art class in an aboveground bunker in Des Moines. The children had been assigned to design effigies of themselves. The teacher had put on a record of Christmas music, though it was not Christmas. The children had had their milk. Suddenly, the teacher reported, they began snipping at their faces. They gashed their hair in chunks. They slit their necks and spoke through the incision. By the teacher's word— herself unharmed—the child's eyes *were not there*. Said teacher serving 25 to life.

2.   PINKING SHEARS—The effect of these on a length of bed sheet. The effect of these on a length of cheek. The effect of these on a length curtains, cream, bird wings, film, your mother. *Where were you? Why did you not answer when I called?*

3.   MOWER BLADES—At some point the earth was air and air was earth and through the earth the blades moved churning, routing tunnels, forming combs, combs in which the young lay rolled in wombs or chewing Crisco, moaning for the moon. These blades were the first that did not cut.

4.   SHAVING RAZORS—They came for us in swarms. Through the strip malls, sung like bees, kissing at plate windows, scratching, making runes upon the arm, derouting feed tubes from mother's babies through and through them, even sometimes making small men's faces clean.

5.   *I DON'T KNOW WHAT THESE BLADES CAME OFF OF—* They were so large. They fell from nowhere (*we can agree to call the sky nowhere…*

I believe we can).
(*Will you please help?*

)
These blades landed on expressways. They crushed the green out of tall young forests that had begun re-growing in the raze.

They knocked the birds off branches and smeared their eggs into the ground. The blades sung with sound of vast incision. The blades filled the store aisles all swum in contained light. In these blades you could see some head reflected, though never quite the one you wear.

The other things that fell—not knives, but liquid—trash, or parts of people—of these things do not ask. There was nothing in this salt mound left to await, even in the most hopeful of the people.

Still, cuffed in the black, what could manage still made their way, all filled with hidden surfaces and blood miles.

There were a billion half-rebuilt homes stuffed in this era. Much of the new houses' construction had been abandoned underway. The land had been annexed, named and numbered, priced, the dirt laced with wire, the trees with censors, streets with poly-buffered trash—a hundred-thousand megamansions lined by stained glass window big as other houses' sides and encrusted with colors that did not quite exist, invented for this house alone   homes with yachts moored in the day room in case someone wished to feel suddenly at sea—*as on the water, I can sleep*—backcracked acts of magic performed in private parlors by computer on marble stage, under neon lights left blinking, blinking—rooms all gathered hard around a hole through which one could look down through the earth, see the shells and shelves it held encrusted, owned—*we own you*—*all of you are all of ours*— rooms each forever spun in spirals and injecting you with speech beyond a skin—walls all old and stuffed with screaming, a cold reminder of who'd they'd held, what could have been inside them—*would be*—*was*—each instant held forever in awaiting for the next to press against it, push it down into the black catalog of the cells of the unseen.

I could go on at what these days were but the truth is I am tired. Would you even believe me if I did? I've spent enough years with my face arranged in books. I've read enough to crush my sternum. In each of the books are people talking, saying the same thing, their tongues slim and white and speckled with the words.

I don't want to be here. I want to get older. I want to see my skin go folding over.

Someday I plan to die.

When I was 1, most nights the house would fill with teeth. They lined the walls and studded the ceiling fans. They would come down like rain and click around my bed. In my head they built a stutter. I couldn't feel my hands yet but there was something then also in me—something gnawing, something come undone.

When I was 2, I licked the sun some. I could spread it open with my fingers. I could tell it what I wanted. I could float further than even that.

When I was 3, the world went flattened and we couldn't find the streets. My arms felt made of tissue. Words woke up inside my head. I would speak them as if I meant to speak them—as if they'd always been all mine— sometimes their grain would cut my stomach—I felt I did not need the stomach—I felt OK.

When I was 4, I remember someone standing above me in the night.

When I was 5, each time I wore white I found myself slowed down. I could see the shapes run out of other's mouths, and I could see their arms ahead of where they were. I could see their faces stretching white with wrinkle and the degrading hue stuck in their eyes.

When I was 6, I found the ground got softer if I rubbed it with my shin. There was a certain part of the backyard where I went straight through into a den. In the den there was a man seated upright in a chair and the man told me exactly what would happen.

When I was 7, I dreamt the names of every child I'd ever have. In the dark I scratched them on my forearms, all fifty thousand. When I woke up my skin was clean, though there were new bruises on my knees.

When I was 8, I ate a tree. It coming back out was the hard part. That year I saw only the turning weather burn through other people's eyes. By now my knees had still not healed, and my blood behind them had turned purple.

When I was 9, I'd buy a new school notebook and get home to find it filled. Often with drawings of myself inside my mother, and often with someone else in me. When I would try to show my mother the pages all became one page.

When I was 10, I don't remember.

When I was 11, I don't remember.

When I was 12, I changed my name. I went by blather. I wouldn't wink unless you knew. My hair went curled. My eyes changed shape. It was only in the dark that I could think.

When I was 13, I don't remember.

When I was 14, I'd hide in bed so many days my skin would stick tight to the sheets—in the end it was the sleep that tore me open. It was soft sleep ate my brain. I met so many men in folds of nowhere—ones I'd found or fucked or scratched the skin on or ate or was ate by or swam with through the ground.

When I was 15, I found a ring and wore it on my thumb. Each day it got a little tighter. I lost one finger, then another. I didn't want to quit the ring. It had my real name writ inside the band. I swallowed it with sugar.

When I was 16, I squirted my first baby as a cuff of creamy cud behind the house. I swear the child had eyes. I worked his girth over with my fingers in the gummy earth, already bubbling, and no matter how hard I packed and patted, I could hear the breathing in my teeth. I hid the patch with nettle. In the morning, the yard was swarmed.

When I was 17, my parents were carried off into the antbed on the hill. I clawed the dirt for hours and all I came back with was this rash. At night the rash would rise up off me and hang above my body. I could hear it speaking in my sleep. I can hear it even now—and now—and now.

When I was 18, the house's caulking swelled. The sky would disattach. It would come to curl around my throat. A little lake welled in my belly. Holes opened up inside the ground. I managed not to have them eat me, even when I went and threw myself on in—as if there were a magic sleeve of cellophane around me—as if I needed to go on. I did not need to go on.

When I was 19, the tone began.

When I was 20, I didn't sleep at all—*such hours*—soon I learned to see the men hid in the eaves—the doors lodged in the séance—the stink.

When I was 21, I met the father—another man who swore he knew—knew what I had in me—knew what I would need. This is what he said. In the night his forehead hid the sky. I woke to blood spots on my pillow, in our oat bran, in the sink drain, but still I stood beside that man—I touched his hands and said the words—we were one then.

When I was 22, I don't remember.

The mother now had given birth twenty-two times since the father's exit five days prior. Each time the span between the births decreased. The pregnancies were swift and brutal. She expelled her paste in gush and crumbs. The warblings of her and the babies' bodies both boomed through the empty rooms around them. Sometimes the mother felt she could have named the ancient human names of all the men that made her bigger, despite the blindfolds, the ice and biting—she could taste them in the branding of her flesh—a permanence mostly lost on the ejections.

Person 2030 had been 811's, who like the mother had descended from two bodies rendered during DELETED ERA. This child—the only one of hers that had thus far survived behind its eyes, held in its cruddy back and black saliva—had been the reason the father left, she knew. Though he'd not expressed this so directly—he'd said nothing really, just been gone—she could tell he'd despised the baby for shucking off his image, for already beginning to grow old. The air had seemed to buzz between them.

The other births after 2030's were a different matter, following a similar structure to the system of her aging, if reversed—one for each year, young and coming, if all crammed into such a short amount of time—the same spiral cut procession seen in all things, of all things one after another—new infants bloating in her as if in instants, spooling ropes on ropes of breathing cells. She tried to hold them in but they came out.

The 2nd child had burst unfurling as a smudge of scum on the black summer pavement tile while the first child crawled through the whole house calling the father's forgotten name, already gone. The stench had been horrendous, like endless fire. 1180 had washed with bleach and light for days and still could not forget. The curd left rashes on her face.

The 3rd child had been a trembling wash of chunks that would not stop running, squashed and ransacked in the eyes. It did have eyes, at least that. 1180 took to wearing diapers or standing over buckets until she stopped caring about the carpet.

The 4th child sluiced out while 1180 stood ironing a work shirt she knew 811 would never need to wear. Even if he returned there'd be no reason. Person 811's place of employment had been converted into pyres. The church was eaten up with acid dust and some white substance. There were no words to call the evenings . And though the counted dead would never end, the state had claimed use of the bodies to build a wall—a wall that would keep them, finally, protected. 1180 ironed anyway. She pressed her knuckles to the iron's steaming eyes to make a memory.

The 5th child came out of the wrong hole during a shit.

The smell of the 6th child—*the mother despised herself for this*—reminded her of biscuit gravy, and that was all she'd eaten then for weeks.

The 7th child grew its voice first and still spoke inside her when she was most alone. The 7th child knew things about her and rose them on her skin in detailed dioramas. The 7th child was not a woman or a man.

The 8th child seemed to want to make it. This child had kept in place for two whole days. By the time it came out as stippled magma, one solid body seared to the lining from where it'd come. 1180 had swelled large as a window. It pulled and pulled at her until after some time in the sun room it did not.

The 9th through 19th child came one after another like rollercoaster cars deformed and farting, hardly gas but so much blood—and then the 20th child emerged immediately thereafter, as a glassy substance the mother could manipulate between her hands—enough to make so many bulbs to light the outside bright forever—enough to build a boat had there been anywhere to row.

The 21st child swam around 1180 and caressed her head and told her future and said that soon 1180 would feel safe and she would have what she'd always wanted, but there was still more things she had to do yet and could she hold on please, could she hold, and 1180 shook her head and tried to turn to see this child, this sweet one, this living sheet, and yet no matter how quick she turned her head or in which direction the child could not be seen.

The 22nd child was made of paper, on which Person 1180 wrote.

The 23rd child, this latest stammer swollen up inside her soon-to-come, flooded the folds inside her with its pre-forming—it felt larger than the others—it already had so many eyes, had already filled in though the sound of everything inside her where among awaiting blood the mother felt the thing she'd meant to be herself learning her veins.

Person 811, somewhere elsewhere, found himself inside a box. The box held a long low light like the kind of light birthed by machines. He could see his short arms crimped with busy muscle. He could see his gushing veins and the scratch marks where he or something else had scratched them. There were scratch marks in the box above his face, bright splinters wedged under his nails.

811 had no idea how long he'd been inside the box. The last thing he could remember was some leaning purple room. From the room he'd moved into an elevator and the elevator sealed. The elevator had descended for several hours and held no music. At times the elevator seemed to be moving to the right or left, or at an angle, or through color. The elevator's buttons were unmarked. He'd kept on trying buttons with one sore finger till one of the buttons knocked him out.

Before the elevator, he remembered standing in a dark froth up to his neck. It'd been too dark inside the air, too, to know where exactly what made what. He'd gone for miles and not found land—though he had found, by feel, among a patch of lubricant, a tiny plastic ring that fit his finger just exactly, though it kept slipping off, a little burning, and soon he lost it back into the depth.

811 felt something else there with him in the box. Something small and fat and grousing near his feet. He could not budge. He could not think of whom to call for. His mind blanked over so many things he'd one time known—his phone number, how long or fat his dick was and how it had fit into other people, the names of any presidents of Where, or of what his insides looked like on the inside—he'd seen his insides, some technician had showed him in a picture once, gushed and brown and wound, he remembered that—he could not think which way was up.

He knew there was someone somewhere wanting, and he wanted to remember. He tried to think of things he'd thought he'd thought before in other days of other years in the idea that thinking them again would make him click back on where he'd been or what he'd done after. He felt his thoughts flop off from him like live fish:

AM I A FIRE?

HAVE I BEEN MURDERED?

WHAT WAS THAT ONE KIND OF BEER I BELIEVED I LIKED MOST?

WHICH ONE OF ME IS THIS THINKING?

HOW MANY FINGERS WOULD I HOLD UP IF I COULD MOVE MY ARM?

The box was getting smaller, longer. The heat grew with his sigh. His face itched. His veins itched. He counted backwards. The other air the box held itself around his head.

Person 811 felt his name nudge somewhere in him, thrumming upward through his lungs: a name. A name. He'd had one. He spoke his name aloud, again, again. He'd known other people had had his name before him but they were not inside him now—not that he knew. He found that in saying his name aloud in certain phrasings he could remember other people who had also said it—his father, his boss, the bank, the heads in nightmares, his wife—yes, he'd had a wife—a what?—a woman. He could almost smell her. He could not remember much else. He also found that if he said his name enough the same way it began to become another name—something much longer and more difficult to pronounce—something deformed from how his tongue went, very old.

Person 811 knew he was not immortal. He had only been left alone by chance—something shitty in his pheromones, a certain chemical in bad cologne, an incantation he'd not meant to let slip the day before by pressing a certain code into his home phone unaware—there was nothing else about him—when he thought about his hand it hurt. In the nights since then, whenever that was, the man had continued turning aged. He had seen the sheen slip out from behind the skin around his face. He had watched his skin and fingers newly droop. Though days were so short by the hour, when strung together, one after another for weeks or years or which however, in those unglassed contraptions, they seemed even fewer. Soon, he was only thinking of long windows on beach vacation homes. He imagined himself standing neck deep in the warm surf, treading sunned.

811 could have spent the remainder of his life inside this box, he imagined. He would not have felt cheated or ill-framed. He felt flashes in his stomach sometimes, squirts of long silent clods of film of time he'd logged and disregarded. Once—he remembered quickly, his body caught taut trying to sit up—along a stretch of blue sod just south of his prior house he'd seen a mile-long pile-up gushed with blood; neck-deep in the blood, the women crying and mosquitoes swarming for the fresh dead and the not dead yet and the mostly healthy—he'd seen the boils on bodies boiling up with blister in the ransacked sun, their voices peeling at the nothing just above them, inscribing light with all their fear, bursting chocolate lather through their eyelids in the pressure and their reams of fast-ejecting babies floating womby on the curdlip; that day after all that he'd gone home and ate cold tacos and fucked his wife and slept all night.

Yes yes, his wife, she was a woman. She had eyes with color and once she'd touched a prism and for years and years she'd been all that he could know.

Suddenly, beyond his thinking, the lid on the air inside the box came off above him. At first there was so much light he could not see beyond the crag of swarming color platelets. He thought he'd gone so deep into nowhere he'd come out the other side.

Soon then room formed in the flush. In the room there was no wind, no other flesh caught by the walls. The room held just the box that held him, as far as he could see. The space lay long and without texture. 811 found that he could move. He felt the blood rush through his sternum. It filled his arms and made them seem as if erasing from the inside.

The father stood up from the box.

Beyond the box he saw then that he'd not been inside a box at all but just there lying on some surface. The floor was wet and somewhat flooded from a liquid dripping from above, through a dark spot puckered on the ceiling, though which he could hear a some kind of semi-human moan—an orgasm or a singing or confusion among sleep, or all of these at once tangled together—and yet the sound seemed to him second nature to the air here, another part of all our manner.

Hung on the wall from end to end and all he saw so many massive pictures, frames of him caught from all those unremembered years, yet in each one doing nothing—just there standing at the lens—nowhere ungone. In each image he looked older—his face looked burned—his cheeks half see-though and covered with tattoos he could not remember getting and which were no longer there still on his face. Up close he even looked worse than ever—the cells destroyed there, filled with jacked up crap like tiny cities. The closer he looked, the deeper periled—populations being ripped apart, maggots screwing on wide white altars, money smothering the trees.

Person 811 felt someone behind him. Someone unnumbered. Someone behind him—behind him—diamond air.

He continued turning but could not make the airspace frame his eyes.

On the flipside of the mirrors in the room that held Person 811, the surface held another room—a long thin room encircling the walls. Inside this room a phalanx of cameras had been arranged to records the innards of the air. The cameras' lenses were wide and curved each as skull-sized globes—they had been used in prior years to record some of the highest grossing cinematic bodies in creation, thereafter replicated on the earth uncounted times.

Upon the father's rising from the box into the twin space—his body already spinning and spinning after something—the lenses' glass began to fog. The glass dripped sweat like human skin and rumpled with the smell of metal burning. The cameras had been designed for this condition. The cameras' makers understood certain things about Person 811—what that number itself meant—who he had thought he'd been, and who he was now, who he had once wanted to be, what he would actually become.

Across the bubble of the lens eyes, a flush of bacteria, made for cleansing, became released. Their tiny translucent tongues absorbed the liquid, became drunk, allowed the screening to stay captured clear. The image of Person 811 continued to hit tape, replicated into planes. The icons wrapped around against each other, stored in spools that rolled in gyration in rooms behind the room where the cameras watched this body move.

Behind the room that held the cameras, wedged between the camera room and the room that held the film, a man stood standing upright in the light there in his flesh without a head. The man did not move or think or want or breathe but the man knew all about the father and the cameras and what had come before them.

In other years, before he lost his head, the man had, at some time or another, been on the inside of every human home. The homes' owners did not know the man, or that the man had been there. From each home the man took just one thing he knew would soon be missed. *I cannot think of what things like those could be now*. He'd swallowed each thing after thorough sucking, to change the taste. The man's intestines were a mess. In certain homes the man would stand over the sleeping people. He'd run his fingers in the drapes. He'd lick the skin off a husband's face, or cry the room full, or kiss the children and braid their hair. Sometimes he'd just stand there inches over, still as glass. Often he'd still be there when the folks woke and yet they went on just the same.

Those years were over now. The man weighed less now. He had a new employment, and so inside that, a new life.

The man could not remember where once he'd had a head that looked exactly like Person 811, who in turn looked exactly like someone else. He, exactly like Person 811, could not remember beyond the placeholder of his knowing how in the time he'd already lived he'd lived through the top times of his life already, and how these other moments, these were after.

They were men made of the same skin, like all men, again.

The man watched Person 811 spin around around around. He watched 811 spread his hands across the blank walls, searching for a seam or knob or some way in.

In his hands the headless man felt the things Person 811 felt.

You would call the feeling *aging*.

He called it *Cone*.

Person 1180 found the way the men had ripped the stuffing out of 811's office walls. They'd shit in the Victrola and smeared the whole of the air with something. They'd overturned 811's black plastic desk. Taped to the underbelly of the desktop were several glossy photos of some woman nude but for a hood. There were markings on her body. 1180 could not tell if they were in the picture or drawn on. For sure someone had traced the woman's nipples so many times with the tips of his fat fingers that the flesh had been rubbed through. The stink of the father's scentless discarded excess semen clung around the woman's image slick like night.

1180's newest wounds had been addressed. She'd absorbed the stinging of the entries of the men into the dark inside her. The scabs were patchy. The men were done and gone and elsewhere for awhile. She'd kept her eyes closed and her mouth wide the whole time. She'd thought so hard into the silent space she carried she could not remember what they'd done—no inch of new wreck stored in her synapses among all the other hell she'd held—though she could hear the newer infant all inside her come alive, thrumming brighter now than any other she remembered, knitting hyper in her skin.

What she did not see did not have to happen, she'd been taught.

Outside tonight the air was liquid. Children and blood and mud or shit clods floated past the window in oblong droves of packets. Occasional tremors like someone choking shook the texture off the home's foundation and its eaves. The tone, for now, was silent, or just perhaps too loud or high-pitched for her to attend.

On TV, 1180 watched the men roll a huge translucent ball along the expressway. Men and goats stationed on both sides watched the procession from behind a velvet cable. At the center of the ball there was a nude woman, strapped with her arms above her head. The women's breasts had been augmented so that they obscured the majority of her torso. Her nipples were so brown they appeared black. The woman's pure white hair had been combed with glitter and bits of foil that made her seem expensive. A large brass band mostly of tubas followed the ball in its procession, squalling basslines uncoordinated from one performer to the next. The men who pulled the ropes that dragged the ball were made up bronze and coiled all in the face like royal bulls.

1180 recognized certain of the men's gashed or pimpled foreheads. They seemed everywhere at once. This had all already happened.

The men grunted though their holes in deformed rhythm as they brought the ball toward the wide bright eye hung on the city. 1180 swam the channels through several hundred angles aimed at different close-ups on the woman's flesh, her eyes blank and elaborate.

1180 could hear the woman's thoughts—the addled feed spoke into her head in a voice like her voice if shifted older and still aging—wholly ruined—the men around her barking and barfing, throwing their fists into the light, around which the whole sky seemed to pucker, and the woman's voice groaned on and on and older still.

1180 could not stand to hear the woman speaking any longer. She felt a button on her tongue, but she'd already pressed it so many times and still felt nothing. The men inside the TV shitting mnemonic cash back and forth between their being. 1180 turned the TV off but it stayed on.

In the kitchen 1180 stood among the way the man had ransacked the storage fridge. The men had eaten all the bee meat and drank the runoff water and the pine bread. All they'd left behind was condiments—countless plastic packets salvaged from fast food, distributed in past weeks by kids in massive trucks with countless turrets and steaming screens. Despite the trucks' clear impenetrability men for miles would crowd around them gnawing and knocking one another's eyes out.

1180 felt mostly calmer after suckling just one packet of the chemic mayonnaise. She experienced feelings of vast euphoria, self worth and creativity, as well as a warm flush feeling through her linings. It tasted like sucking on a baby doll but it was easy. Several hours without imbibing caused withdrawal, the inverse symptoms of which included ranting, loss of wisdom, megalomania, frothy discharge from the ears.

1180 tried to keep herself in hunger as long as possible but most days she gave in quick—she could feel the hole growing inside her, a round hole lined with even wider teeth.

1180 saw by the large panel LCD clock that had been installed in her forearm that it was time to go downstairs. Everyday from 1 to 4 was MANDATORY SPONSORED INTERMISSION, a practice the state had instituted in the house for several weekends in the months before the presence of the present child. Each home or house in the local area had been installed with safety stairwell bunkers for a cost absorbed in the aggregate war effort—the war against the long black dogs—the war against the books that had not yet been read—the war against the war against the prisms installed in our ribcages—the war against Kentucky's buried growling—the war against anyone named John. Each war went on regardless of when it ended or began, and should be feared beyond the fear of fearing any other dead idea.

The INTERMISSION method was intended to increase tranquility, introspection and to avoid the most common hours of disease—the air panes ripping, helicopters dropping from the sky, spokes of bugs forced through the air vents, paper growing legs and standing up, none of which she'd felt the sound or tremor of an inch of, though this was entirely the point—and but mostly during that time, when they had shared it, 1180 and 811 cowered in the practice position invented and taught wide by the state. 811 would cover his head and babble in a pretend female voice. 1180 kept asking that he repeat what he said louder so she could understand, but 811 would only close his eyes and bleat.

1180 could not remember anything at all or else about 811 ever near her in his life beyond the rich reeking of shit thickening in his pants in various terror, goosey spillage writhing down in long lines for the stairwell where 811 hid and begged against the nothing that had come. And 1180 loved this man regardless. In the night asleep she said his other name.

The safety stairwell, as far as they'd found, led to nowhere. It went on and on into the plastic of the earth. The air seemed sticky and filled with mirrors. Just before he disappeared, 811 had claimed to have continued down and down until he'd found a little coffee shop that sold cold crumpets, but 1180 knew this was a sham—he'd only meant to set her mind at ease. In his time, at times, for some lengths, he had been so thoughtful of her, such a man.

In her own time with the stairwell alone, for all her walking, the mother had developed muscles all throughout her—tremendous calves in which she could see her sheen of beef having seemed to develop the same contoured expressions as a face. Even now, in the mandate's remission, she still practiced the practice each afternoon at the learned time, though mostly she waited until the child fell sleeping, as the intermission stairwell's deformed and deforming air did not seem something he or she should breathe.

During the year of nonstop rains, before the burning, the stairs had flooded up a pool inside it some flights down, which in the night—*the mother did not know this*—the father once had tried to swim down into it. He'd seen a glowing in the depths there, some kind of light sometimes as if from reflective metal money, sometimes as if from one large blinking pupil. He had not been able to swim down far enough—his small lungs red as if to ripping—the pressure in his head like large hands—he'd given up.

1180 had not told 811 she'd used the water in the stairwell to wash their laundry, and her body—she'd had no choice—nothing was coming through the home's pipes to their rooms, none to wipe the baby clean or mix with liquor. The stairwell water seemed like any other water for the most part, though it was so cold and somehow slick, and sometimes she felt sure she could feel it staying specific through her holes, not mixing with the other liquids of her body, private rivers. So many things they kept from one another without a reason.

Some days 1180 would come to sit by the water's lip and read. She read mostly instruction manuals for dead appliances and convoluted diagrams of local zoning, as there were no other words these days created—too many were too defeated, and all remaining paper had all been reserved by assholes for phonebooks, receipts and bills. The moan of the minor ocean contained inside their building made her calm, gave her somewhere to escape the flux of massive sunlight that 811 had to walk into every morning to get paid—employed, as were most men before it'd been abandoned, to build the Universal Roof. It was hard work. He came home each day covered in blood, little smear marks around his eyes where he'd kept crying to keep his cheeks clean so he could see. It made the father weary and irritable, hard to love.

In her small evenings by the strange water there, the mother had seen people held under the surface—flattened faces with no eyes, or with more eyes than one should want to have, or in the place of eyes, advertisements— they were in there, underwater but alive. She saw men with tongues so long that they could lick themselves in several pleasure places—she saw lardy machines of vast dimension like no object of this air—she saw whole hotels or office buildings of other bodies coming rising from the bottom, men in every window making gestures, women writhing on the beds behind them, surrounded by machines. They could see her through the surface, clawing at it. She could hear their bloating in the night.

The mother breathed. Something on the stairwell now seemed to row the air around her, as if shifting. The walls seemed closer than she last remembered, the faces of the steps much thinner.

Behind her eyes were also stairwells, which also led to something gone.

The mother fumbled down along the stairwell reeling, feeling at any moment ready to go toppling headfirst, though somehow keeping her posture aimed in weird momentum by dragging her arms out beside her in a thin X on the air.

At some point the walls became so close together there was no space at all between them, and yet she walked.

The mother went down and down. The surface of the air seemed to suck around her. She found herself head-on, faster and farther. She could not stop her body coming with it. She opened and her eyes and closed her eyes and opened them and watch the pattern of the texture change: like the language in the book she read the child would, the same symbols in her lids. Without seeing, she went farther down along the stairwell than she'd ever before been—past the bit of wall on which she had meant to mark her future child's arriving height—past the bit of wall that'd crumbled open and through which she could not see, but could reach her arm up to the elbow—past the low water mark even, where the water had once sat still and teeming, waiting for its next fit of rising—she felt nothing. She went so deep beyond the house there was no air—the dark around her held together chalky, ashen. She could no longer measure her impression of her descending of the stairs. She slipped and twisted in the darkness but there seemed no context to it, no dimension—as if she'd woken up inside a pillow full of dust, the grain clung in her throat and whites of eyes. She fought to find a ledge or other landing to the space there while in the dark she sunk straight down—not quite free falling, but growing lower, ground in amongst sand. She felt it chewing at her knees and cheeks together. She opened her mouth to call out for someone—*who?*—and in the dry dump her cheeks bloomed empty with fat pits. The gums inside her ate the language. She could feel her shoulders ripping up. Her fingernails seemed to pull out from their sleeves. It pulled all through her.

The mother vomited a bird. First there was one bird, then there were many, their tremble rummaged up her middle, from her throat. They scratched her cheeks and pore meat with their clawing, her O-hole stretched wide as it could go. Enormous birds, she saw, as white as nowhere, thrushed with feathers matted in a gel. They kept coming up out of her in a chain, all gushing and aflutter—*silent*—each one imprinted all through and through their gristle with a word, one word for each all written in their linings and down the contours of their suits, the word and word again all densely textured, though the mother could not read the words as they emerged— she could not make out the letters or what about them, or their presence there at all. Each bird's word was its own word for it alone, though all their screeching came out of them the same, brief and lame and hellish.

Once emerged, the birds stayed thick around her rushing, flapping fat, their gross warped wings beating at her body, pulling her back up out from the fold. She felt their enmassed cluck-caw on her eardrums and their blown motion somehow muffled into one continuous barrage, their note-stung tendons pulsing at her hot as if after some way through her body there back in, finding none—altogether in their presence wanting someone other than she was.

The sky above the house began to blink—the tone surrounding as it stuttered as something again soft inside it came apart and lathered down on us in waves—old fires burning still in all the houses and phantoms fucking—the air all written full of what any evening left alone must do and always would.

Somewhere elsewhere hours or days later, *she could not tell and did not think to try to*, Person 1180 found herself inside a box. There held a long low light like the kind of light along a longer hallway, someone in a far room glowing with TV. Her skin was so thin that she was see-through, held inside her, her organs putty colored and dented in. Her blood curled through the corridors like tangled instruments between. There was language cut into the box above the mother's face. She could not read. She had no idea how long she'd been inside the box, or how the box was any different from any hour held before or coming after. She could not remember her number or anything about any room. There was a rumble spinning through the flat panes. At some points, through glass, the mother saw some of the men who'd filled her up, or who she had seen inside their eyes how they had meant to. Some of the men were holding infants, and those were eating. *What were they eating?* Some of the men were exactly her. Each time she closed her eyes the box was still right there, its darkness burning.

Person 811 moved toward the polished wall. Tucked in the far corner there, under a small sheath of black protective plastic that burned his hand, he found a panel that instead of showing outward, opened in. Through the panel, he could see a bulging naked woman standing in another house. She was pretty, he thought, beyond the lesions. She was ...

Person 811 stood with one hand spread at the glass panel over the woman, stroking with his thumb and his ring finger the raspy spread of where her body breathed. The woman's eyes were closed and kept on closing—innumerable lids. Her gut was stacking up at each new instant with fat in fat like pyramids. An ageless dark rouged through her shape tracing her veins. His tips ached where he could not remember before that he'd touched her, and not the other way around. Other men before him had left their mark there on the glass from the same rubbing, though the father could not smell them or defer—he could only taste the itch of it.

Against the screen he laid his head and heard the shrieking.

Before I was born inside the mother I slept inside the wound for 37 years

There was a spot between the gloss and sill where I would settle in and suck the dust

My mother's hull had many doors wedged in her knees and neck, her belly

You could slit the locks with one wet thought

I could not count the other women hid among the mother though they filled me turn by turn with sight

For a while I was the women too: I had husbands, blisters, monthly blood of those I had not nurtured

I had bumps all across my scalp, one for each of whom I'd wanted or would awake in wanting soon

I was the child

I as well often was the mother and the father, though they did not have my hands

Nor did I want what hands I had been given

When I slept I dreamt only ever of the Cone

The years went on like that for years

Sometimes what a year was would change in midst of counting

A month would pass and it'd been a week

An hour did it's thing and it'd been twenty

The space of air outside my mother often filled with dogs

Or it would fill with larvae or with flowers

Some days other men or sounds of men

Inch by inch I watched the years that were not years sludge along under motor oil and ash

What white of wide machines among me scratching rooms and windows into all my eyes

Our hole of god

I heard the evenings counting down

What had been and always be had not yet happened

Inside the house my mother hung long reams of paper, which rats would rip down to use for dens

There were the walls we had repainted

One fresh coat for every layer of our flesh

For weeks while we were sleeping the skin would become costumes, helmets, rings on fingers, fat sacs, gloves and gowns, by lengths destroyed, unveiled

In these guises we would walk around and feel the world

Inside the fold I learned to read by staring at an afghan my mother's mother
hemmed from old clothes in her rivulets of sweat

The grunt of something peeling

Dadmeat

Money

I was already very old

I learned to write by pinching gristle in the cortex of my face to kill the
instant as it happened

For each face I held for hours some nights there were several other faces I
would feel behind the one I knew is mine

I did an eating in me

I shat me out again

I made out of my shit another chest

I made my skull inside the mother

I called it *me*

Then I forgot

I learned to read again the new tongues by counting money where it was
placed against our frame

We were laid upon white tables

My mom and I and anybody else at all I had not ruined

I learned to laugh by buying land

The land outside my forming body was named by hours full of light

I loved this light's age, from this distance

I did not need another way

I had just only pieced together my cerebrum and the gorehouses of my wanting one night when in the blood someone reached and took me by my arm

My joint slipped from its socket

The arm inside my arm went numb

Among me on the air my mother screamed as if she'd hit her head against some low ceiling

As if what was coming out was not how she'd expected or intended

And what was all this white foam

Why the putty on her nostrils

In the color of the Cone

It had always been this way already

I did not want to come out of her either

I was miles long and so was she

I knew all of what had been done in the Cone's name and in my name by me and all the other men, where a man is also any woman, any summer, any inch

I did not want to see the me who I'd already been always awaiting

What one of me I'd let touch and rub my buttons in the middle of my grossness

I tried to use my nails, full grown already, to claw my way back to where I'd hid

Her soft tunnels streaked with rip and all those rooms there

It did not work

At least at last I left my itch imprinted on her insides, a gluey stamp on our last life

When I came out fully finally I found my mother held inside an axis above the floor

Her gut still hung fat once I had emerged as with me in it

All the bruises on her face

We did not touch

There was an air there cogitating

It is like this even now

Even now, I mean, there is still something here about the gleam about me
I do not like

And still again

One thing about my birthing fingers is they came equipped with rings

No gems, just bands of plastic

When I make them spin they burn

My veins bulged as if hiding something solid in them

Look out the window

Who is there

Who is it inside me I can't quite feel

As when my mother eats a sandwich—no bread no butter—dust

I can't keep myself from snatching at it, after more growth

I can't restrain the tremor in my life

My even longer nails now making marks to match the ones set inside her

Sets in sets of parallels unsized

My mother in the evenings walks room to room with her eyes closed, a necklace painted on her neck, a blistered dictionary

This house runs in all directions from itself

I can feel the walls tug in the kitchen, all air so stung with thinking, neon white

The night cut brighter now than wherever you are

And the dawns are even worse

I do not want to go on making more of me in my own mind

I have not in some time eaten dinner or laughed a little

Hang on, there's someone else that wants to talk

Hi

I am the child inside the child

I have another child inside me

That child has another child inside that child with another child inside it also

I also am the mother and the father also and I also am the child around my child and etc.

I'm exactly like the Cone but very different

Like you but different

So

So inside one of all these children, in their lining, the lining of the lining, there is a cyst

The cyst is made of cells of skins of other bodies in other years before my mind before I died

Before all of anyone forever

Inside the cyst there is a tumor & inside the tumor there is a clasp

The clasp will scream and rattle when you touch it—*it is yours too*—it speaks a voice of many men

The men are hungry, as you are hungry

Do not be afraid

Undo the clasp

The fold will open

Blood will be singing in the tone

The sun inside the sun will bow

Fold your arms into a gesture you remember

Move into the fold

The manner of your movement once in the there again depends on several
factors I don't have the compassion to explain

Regardless, you will enter, and you will see the day

You will begin

Inside the fold locate the fold again

This other fold can open also

Move into this fold, too, when you find it

If you find it

And I believe you will

Though you are relatively young

And this might go on for many hours, or even winters

Ages of dead sun

By now you will feel a great exhaustion

Something screaming in your wads for our life

Inside the fold inside the fold you will see someone is waiting

Many of us

Endless people without their face

People you held known once, all of them stuttered

Soon there will be more

Person 811 had gone so far into the fold of other air now he could see no way going back. He remembered the mirrored room and all the buzzing. He remembered putting his head one certain way against one mirror, in which his face there reddened, and then grew—the distance between him and himself there coming closer—*what was this looming*—and how as he came to touch his head against the mirror, he'd moved his eyes straight through his eyes. He even remembered the hot compressed feeling like something punched to tattoo flesh that seemed to metastasize all through his body each time while inside his eyes he blinked him through.

What he did not remember was how he'd lost his way. From the mirrored room he'd come into a color: unprismatic, globbing, old. As he'd moved forward, sideways or simply down, the color seemed to change. When the room went hyper-red the air was liquid and he had to swim to save his breath. He'd slashed his thin arms through the lukewarm potion. He'd kicked until he found a wall—a flat clear wall that spread in all directions.

Through the wall he saw a child—someone standing just outside the plastic skewed with eyes large as fifty fathers—eyes that grew into other space— rooms where he could see people he knew and had known, growing, eating, making fuck. He felt his body try to shout out through the pane to make it open, to thread himself into this once familiar air, but then the holes making the child's eyes had blinked and fleshed in and moved away. In the place his voice had been inside him, then the water moved to fill his skin. The father felt caverns crumple in him. He felt his lungs expand. As he gasped the slipping liquid he found himself lodged in creamy whir—the blue of blues set ringed in more eyes—he felt them itch. The eyes were looking at a fire. A horrid burning, miles and miles, clot and cinder sticking to his wetness. He felt some massive eyelash cragged at his slits, his him in he here. The eye flipped shut and again open.

BLINK

The sound the blinking made inside him came like someone sawing on the air, like metal melting into metal—though on the outside of his body, had someone been there who could hear it, it sounded like no sound.

The color changed again—his person with it. He spun around. There were all these versions of him crowded around, as far as he could see, some slouched, some sick or burning. They were all looking straight on into his mind, teeming hard for clear transparence in the ways he had seen himself become, ways in.

He put his hands over his face and screamed for someone to come swimming up into himself and make him move, to fill his body with fresh flesh.

BLINK

He appeared inside a barking dog—*this was the dog he'd heard out his house for every year he lived, every year, no matter which house, the same barking, the same evenings.* In the dog he moved through its body as its barking, moved out of himself to hover over the dog's skin, where he could see through saw not far-off window his own body sitting there inside the light, and just as his body began turning to look at him, *his twin eyes spinning*, He (in the barking) turned back to air and became inhaled into the same dog body once again.

BLINK

He burned inside the cracking meat on the black pan hot as some summer—*a summer made of sound, in which the whole world had took to spinning faster, throwing bodies off it into no light*—in the meat his body began releasing liquids he had had once imagined gone forever—sweat and shit and spittle, semen, tears—and with these his flesh was basted, charring his flesh into new flesh, into flesh he could not recognize himself in, though he could smell the frying of his panic, and he could sense the searing down into him of what he had been, and what he'd wanted to be, what he'd done. The blackened body was then eaten, administered into another body, flooded through a bloodstream, through certain organs, which transferred his person into heat—as heat he vibrated in vocal cords of the voice the body carried, which sounded like his own fully, he heard himself saying his name—

BLINK

He appeared in the background flat of a famous painting on a wall in room inside a mall somewhere now mostly buried under earth, buried and still there, the blood of all the past and future shoppers holding him in its pigments waiting to be painted in or painted over there again.

BLINK

Nothing.

He was so soft.

BLINK

Hundreds of thousands of bodies copulating in piles of flour, candy, cash, grinding rinds and stumps of self against the next couple in the series splayed unwinding on a mask of sand and dirt spread wider than his eye could manage, there at their center, bellies bulging, and above them all at once, the shrieking field.

BLINK

He appeared in a billion forms of glass—in mason jars slick with men's spit, standing over the father's childhood bed as he lay sleeping—in the carved décor of some crushed carousel, its cracked crank music dead and waiting—in compacted eons of old light—glass in telescopic rifle lenses used to kill—glass in someone's window flat and breathing, through which the person on the other side could not see. Each inch of glass refracted other of him into fifty and into each of those again, splitting hard down through his centers, and his centers' centers, and the mink of days becoming something held. A hard rub in the teething. Him growing young

BLINK

BLINK

BLINK

In the blinking between blinking there was so much he could not count—so many small minutes, hours, he had taken in unknown, collared through his meat. Cold hours came on rolling.

BLINK

He washed up on a white sea where years before he'd taken his wife to dine in a high restaurant where the food was mostly grease. He'd spent so much money that evening so that they might remember one another in this way. They said into each other's faces reams of quite specific words. They'd held their fingers into signing poses. There were other people in the room. The mouths made sounds of spasms. The skin of sky above their heads was bending down. Then upon the sea again, without color, he fell out of himself to no remains. Instead, there on the black shore, was another dog, *the same dog*, though this dog now had no legs. The beach seemed turning unhorizontal. The dog rolled and grunted at him, tried to find a way to grunt himself along the sand. He watched the dog inch away from him, the water washing in over their heads.

BLINK

Someone was tinking on the glass.

A cold eye rummaged in his sternum.

Blowholes.

BLINK

He reappeared inside the house there with his wife—Person 1180—he recognized her—she did not know—he was just behind her, back to back, so that neither could quite see with eyes the form they felt—though they were touching—there was some kind of light flexed through his body— *ah*—a light went off and on again then—when she turned around he was not there.

Who was that? he shouted into the air around him, fraught with black laughing, though where the words were there was sand, and each grain of the sand was him repeating each word we'd ever found, strings of syllables crammed between the Cone and its unending ending, the coming instant at which the words would close and there would be no more said beyond the blinking in the blinking in the blinking in the blinking in the...

BLINK

The father threw up in his hands.

In the throw up, had he looked there, he would have found a map of all of where he'd been, but there was so much other crud covering it over, so much hair and wet and dark black eggs.

Back in the house, Person 1180 appeared coiled on the carpet flexed and stuffed. She did not realize she'd been gone for several days—*days which in the house did not last so long—in which a league of moths had stuffed down the chimney and now were building more space in their sleep—in which someone had come to the door and knocked and knocked and buzzed the bell in patterns and begged and cried into the keyhole.*

In her absence 1180 found the light the house held had brightened by degrees. She could see soil and crap and crystalline things crawling off in corners of the room she'd never noticed rounding out the space—new indentations in the hull. She felt years younger and a little dizzy. Her belly bulged larger than she remembered it'd last been. She was naked and had not been naked as she last recalled. She had been wearing a long blue gown as big as the whole house, stuffed all throughout it. There was something else inside her now. She pinched her chub and felt a lurch along the lining, murmuring like shafts. Her gush caked on her neck all full of speech.

She took turns sitting in the seven chairs around the kitchen table looking for the one that held her well, the one that made her sit straight. Having found the perfect chair at last some evenings later she did not sleep or close her eyes. She held her smile. Inside her head she made calls to every old phone numbers she could still remember and breathed into every silent, paused machine.

The mother could hear the baby screeching from upstairs as the tone's latest long stroke dissolved around her. She kept trying to run to help her son but instead she felt her body going backwards. Several times she ran into the kitchen's plate glass window, through which a mob of pure white dogs had gathered and were milking up a lather. She popped one of the panes out with her elbow on accident and immediately the dogs flew lapping at the fracture. On their breath she smelled her own breath but interlaced with blood. The child's voice bruised the inner layer of the mother's head. She closed her eyes.

She had to imagine she was moving the wrong way to make herself go toward the child.

Upstairs she found the baby had stretched and fattened, its belly bulged as if also pregnant, the skin stretched on its head an unlit bulb. Several birds had convened around the child and were pecking at his flesh—the same white birds from the stairwell, made of language, though she could no longer remember from where they'd come. She had no idea how birds had gotten inside the house and upstairs to the child as the nursery's doors were locked, the windows held unshattered, sealed, the air vents blocked with grate and wire. From small holes in the birds a shrieking waffled in the white webbing of their muscle and their lard.

She grabbed the axe Person 811 had hung over the bedside—*their boy would be a fireperson someday, he swore—when the fire station opened up again—if it opened—it would—it would open—there always would be fire.* She chopped and ripped among the air. She squawked back at the birds in their same voices, surprised at how authentic she could sound. She chased them out into the hallway. Their wings knocked divots on the walls. They shit behind themselves in long leagues, streaking wet white mountains into the mother's hair that caught loose feathers like a skin. The stink made the mother see double, then double double, like a lyric. The room began unveiling. There were so many birds inside the house and always had been.

She swung and swung the axe at all the air there hitting nothing. She threw it down and used her free arms then to scoop the birds down into her from the air, to press in clumps the thrumming meat against her thick chest, the milk inside her turning hard—the birds spreading out around the rind of her now from the outside speaking in.

The mother returned some hours later to the bedroom to find the child grown even larger, heavy white. He'd sat up on the fat crib mattress, fresh with bloodburst. As she rushed forward in the room to smooth and touch him, the child moved his hands across his face as if to hide, but really hide—not the gamey crap-move the mother and her boy had not yet had the chance to play in fun, but truly, to make as if he wished he were not there—as if now he mistook the mother as well for one of the long, winged things that had come at him—as if there were some other place he could move into beyond the room behind his skin. She prayed into the child's ears in the book's language. She kissed his lips and called him son.

She fed the baby frozen cream. He could not keep it down. He puked and puked it. She tried and tried and the baby's eyes just went on caught with old spin. She wiped the child's suddenly enormous forehead. In the child's eyes she could see something moving even when the air between them blurred.

Person 1180 carried the dish of regurgitated milk spew into the kitchen and stood with it there before the window. Having come up from the child, the chocolate sheen had turned a little moldy. My growing baby, she heard herself think. She stirred the sputum with her finger, felt something rising.

She couldn't crush her urge. She ate the pukey ice cream and felt it slide inside her. She threw it up again. She ate it down and threw it up again. She ate it down and threw it up again. Each time the color changed what it came back out as. Each time going in it had new flavor. She had been to college once. She'd kissed a man she'd seen on the TV. She put the ice cream inside the microwave and watched it melt in sputtered waves, watched it evaporate, become dust. Now the room felt very small.

In the child's head his cells were spinning—his pupils wide with what inside or outside him must arrive.

Through the evening the mother slept hugging her chest. The child had stretched so much in several hours he fit a full man's shape exactly. She'd tried to coddle the child, breastfeed him full of her again there through his now large mouth, but he refused to stay in bed. He still smelled like the birds. He paced the rooms downstairs and smoked long curls of his own hair—he ate the melting crap plastered behind the peeling wallpaper, *his stomach snarled*—he sometimes would walk along and on into the wall still there as if unseeing where the house had ended and he was held. The warts and ulcers already broiling up from his sternum would seize and pop in little rhythms.

1180 felt afraid. She saw an age reflected in the full-sized infant's eyes— hardly infant's now—*were they?*—she could not relay contact. She did not know what had come into the son to make the scaffold of his creature.

From some short distance, she would have surely mistaken him for 811—sometimes she did regardless—her body sometimes burned. Through long afternoons she locked her door and stayed in the bed watching the ceiling—waiting that it might crack open and offer her a way. She licked the pictures taken of her and the gone man gushing together before the son, *in that old air, then*, and she stuck them to her body that they might sink in and reconvene.

Through the vents and at the door crack she heard the child moving through the house. In his sudden, swollen body he'd grown violent. She heard him screeching into nothing, throwing chairs or cracking glass, and when the tones came—much louder now, more frequent—the son howled in texture harmonizing. In other silence, she heard him speak in his new gouging voice. The words bulged in strange syntax, like the book and birds and something other, a shape contained by false edges, beyond air. She could feel certain of her son's words grow large and move to bang against the air around her, as if with arms. So much speech coming out of the child's holes—words he'd be meant to distribute over time, which now needed catching up and phrasing. The house's oxygen strained and clung. The syllables and slurring shook the small walls as 2030's tongue and lips grew more and more into their own shape. Not knowing what they knew there, but speaking nonetheless.

The mother wrapped herself in blankets. She felt afraid somehow of growing young, having to see all of this repeated—as if the age the child had gathered in so quickly had been supplanted out from her—she was

much closer to the end than him, her meat insisted. She rolled in the sheets
and comforters and pillowcases and old afghans someone old had knitted,
pounds and pounds of threaded fiber, sunk with sweating among slept
years—under their weight she felt she lost her body into mushing, yet she
could always feel her head, and she could not quite make her eyes close.

Behind the wall the room that held the film that held the father began to grow so great in mass it warped with heat. It made the walls expand and stick to nothing. The floor squealed in juicing ridges full of pulp. The film had grown so thick among its spools that it began to form in knots and spots of blue emulsion. 811 felt himself become melted with it as it grew gathered.

The machines began to smoke. It stunk of burning sweat. The air itself began to grow.

The man without his head and yet still somehow eyes saw the machines steaming from through the wall. He crossed the room toward another wall parallel to the one through which the film room held the father. On this wall he spoke into a set of holes shaped like a star. Someone spoke back to him, in wrecked language. The symbol of the star slightly changed shape. The man without a head might have wished to nod. Instead he crossed the room again halfway toward a third wall against the outdoors, the sun and fields there. In the center of the wall he felt along the surface for a panel till it clicked. He opened the panel and pressed a button. A small hole in the film room with the father opened. The slurring film there began to thread out through the crease—through the crease into the air outside and into the air of all other things—there was a sound of skin or skins becoming slid from—cells barfing wide into the light.

The film spooled out around the building that held the room that held the father. It crept in wadding tides along the flat walls and out into the larger air, fluttered in thin ropes of darkened frame-hid color both all through the make of space and to the ground. It masked the windows of the building where heads had looked in or out on where they stood behind the pane divided. It knocked large birds out of the sky, dark bodies that as they fell dropped many eggs in clots of bombing, their half-bred babies also gone. The film gave sound in popping bubbles, scratching the surface of the concrete miles around the center of its eye. The concrete had been poured by state-named men to cover the earth over and keep all the crap and bugs and bodies or their sound from coming up—the concrete had been poured over rivers, statues, flowerbeds, and homes where homes had been before our homes now, ages interred—encasing the encased. The film slit slots in the fresh ground and went into it, spreading roots. Somewhere deep inside there it found itself again and reconnected in new frame, the father's images rubbing in incidental friction. Through the film could squirt no light.

The film amassed around the building and mussed up quickly, building the building into some sort of slick and massive hive. From a distance the sheen of the film would reflect so much sun though you could not see—it would burn your eyes out—it would want to.

The film grew even as it burst. It grew as babble lathered in computers and as confluence under hair and tideless ocean. The film lashed across continents unseen, gushed in making new memory of its own presence, bowled over forests, wrapped through windows, undid locks. It mummy-wrapped the dead, engorged the subway system stalled and fat with bodies swollen from waves of heat, flossed the teeth of several living. As excrement it wormed into cows and birthed their young, came through TV screens and PC monitors and out through books, splashed up from coffee and other burning liquids, became tongues, became the language the tongues vibrated—it filled every inch of air of certain rooms, of certain weeks already passed and weeks uncoming. In many of the rooms the film came into there was no one left but this did not stop the film's advance.

The film defeated sleep. It wedged as a disease into the ears of the half-conscious, wiped the goggled colors all to white, the motion there embedded back to nothing.

The bodies all woke up. The bodies moved from their beds and touched the window, looked for who had been there and who was coming. The bodies could not see beyond several feet, as if they'd remained stuck their in their own heads, their vision squashed and remaindered in the brain.

The film slid down the mouths of crying babies in their beds or in their cages, left alone in houses squashed by mice deformed and starving. The tape made loops inside their gut. The tape masked their eyeballs, made bandannas, curled into a new shining second skin. *Became the child.* The tape choked the elderly, slapped the deaf. *Became the child.* It washed through sound not known, layered in years of melted vinyl, it stroked the ceiling of soundstages, it skewered the holes in certain kind of breakfast cereal and then ate the breakfast cereal and then repackaged the breakfast cereal in better boxes, boxes more apt to get someone to touch it—*had there been people shopping in these aisles.* It replaced the definitions of certain words in dictionaries no one would ever open. It congealed in the next thing we would bite. It squished in trash compactors, snapped their gears and turned them pudding. *I don't know where we are.* It became the stuff of pancake syrup. It meshed in the insulation of old houses, through the wires, it wore a buzzing, it caused long rips in old maps for new roads new zones new plate tectonics that would burp and screech, that would slide to one side or the other and let some new stretch burble up—*on these flat pieces of new land were other buildings with no windows and no door, inside which there were men or women with no faces, features, no names, no nothing but keyholes in their eyes.*

The film fed into projection booths of theaters no longer attended but still running, their smashed gray light gushed wrong and endless against the biggest walls of smallish rooms, the rows and rows of empty chairs all aimed as if to have even the air itself pay heed—*to see.* The film rolled in and made replacement of all the film on all the shelves in all the shops, all the men and all the women in and on and around the silent houses around any house, *all the same house*, the air of years and years of shapes embedded, forms recreated in grainy grain again, stored in a billion minds a billion times, or something, each sentence spoke a certain way, the way the eyes of certain actors would linger on the camera, the folds of days and age and light composed in each scene—*never again*—the reels and reels of names caught white on black or vice versa—all of this erased—all of this made of the father now—all as the tape spurted off and slithered, as the tape, unknown to the father, squirmed its grabbing girth around what had been and was the world.

That night the shrieking tone really erupted. The house stood on its side. The fibers in the house's rooms erected from their expanses, spindling the hallways with weird fur. The tone went so large it bashed past hearing and into nowhere, *colorlessness*, then back to loud—so strong it popped blood vessels in the child's eyes while he was sleeping—all he saw when he woke again was masked in pillowed red. He didn't mind.

The tone ripped the mother's clothing against her body through the seams, her skin smashed patchy with the resounding tenor, thin bloodshot lines creased through her flesh—spraying the lining of her innards with the spittle of cracking meat, stirring the remainders of what had gathered in her womb there into pigments, changing its face—*a living mush of no known name*. It brought the house's eaves down, cracked the mantle, splashed the windows back to sand, braided the long hairs on the carpet, from the bodies. It peeled the wire out of the hallways, blanched the shutters. It slid its incision in most all things until air itself was hardly there, the night corralled to skeins of dust.

Inside the house, the rooms went warbly and became several rooms at once—where in them people laid on long beds laughing, the light of no moon strumming their nude and something flexed where nothing was. On the air you could see pilling, tiny spindled segments of the seconds split into hyphae, kaleidoscopic cells. The rooms reconvened then, and seemed to lift a little, becoming slurred in as the tone rummaged through the windows of each blink—the reconditioned post-stink stirring of each of these rooms and what they'd held, what they were holding, what they would hold now in the way of some new condition—all there scrambled or erased.

There was a shaking then. There was a long rip, coming from one direction then another. There were a million little tones. You couldn't even hear it—as it began it had always been—the sound of something larger than the whole earth. The tone burped through light and carved it well into a strobe that in repetition appeared to slow down to gone again, while the day shook in the pummel of one thousand drums, the light around it breaking at the knit, pulling anything that had lived longer than it all apart.

When the air again was silent, the mother and the son found themselves outside the house. Where the house had been was mostly nil. Some of the wires that had once held the house down, connected—power, TV, sound, heat, air, telephonic, light, breeze, monitor, alarm—spread sprayed in worming threads up toward the skylight dome nodule that had been installed above the house for weather interpretation. Their fibrous fraying zapped electrons and gave off heat, making cursive on the air. There were rutted suggestions of where the house's rooms had been—weight, impression, space, regard—but the rooms themselves were no longer there.

The mother watched the newly grown child—bigger than her now, a thing she could not carry, ever again—he stood in the air where the den had been, wielding a remote. Though the TV—*or whatever else the remote had controlled*—was no longer there he stood there staring like it was, stroking buttons to err the channel, raise the volume, on or off. She felt some kind of recognition in this action. She shook her head until it fell away. She went and took Person 2030 by his cold forearm—*so thick she could not make her fingers go around*— she felt him rip away. She watched him hulk his hands and stamp the ground with clumsy footfalls, cutting holes into the home's foundation, from which long thin animals reeked and surged, spouting up from where they'd hidden there inside the earth the very instant 2030's presence popped an exit. She could not believe what all had been underneath them all those hours, what other space inside the musk of earth there was, and now above them where the air above the house had come apart. Long claps of gross wind hung combed over through long stunted portholes chafing sections of other air entirely mostly discolored or strapped with lines. The state had ordered an apparatus around the larger sections, a scaffolding made of semi-transparent polymer—so as to preserve the vast billboard horizon, they said, *no eyesores*—though you could still see the outlined shape of what was made. A maze, a bent-up aero-ghetto, half-abandoned in its make, the long braches of corridors meant to place order on the shifting shit sky left undone by the mass death of city workers, men like her disappearing mate—they'd begun falling from their ladders, out of skyscraper windows, thrown from trucks, choked by their ties or other costumes, the interstate spun to knots—whole long strips of street once connecting cities now rewired into loops, crammed with battalions marooned cars, sweltered with the bloated bodies of those who could not find a way to climb down, who spent their last days licking the crumbs up from the dash of where the light hid among the sky.

In some places now, hung on the half-assed aerial architecture, men huddled hidden, using their pants for roofs or flags, the mother saw. Whole colonies had jimmied nooks into the new air, thought most of them, by now, were dead. Others just hung on awnings, apses, little outhung nodules to which they'd tied their necks and jumped. Grappled and grappling. Fat with mucus. Getting groaned. Even without the want, the news would tell you, one could wither through exposure in almost no time, now, with the way the sun could just come on. Count your minutes. Stay inside.

STAY INSIDE, the nation's mantra.

Our house, motherfucker, the mother said aloud into the larger light, *is gone*.

In her own face reflected in the milky leather of what that destroyed space she saw the lines she'd been made of all these years there worked or wormed, each readjusting in the seared meat. There was the bruise still on her neck's bulb from where when she was nine she fell into a hive. The bees had stung her all in the same place, one after another, ignoring all her other flesh; she had swollen that day to an enormous size, but no one else had noticed. Here she was again. Here was her neck now slushed to bands of wriggle, strummed in black chords by the hands that had grown up in her gut—her gut as gushed and gobbling as the thing inside her spread into her, was her, wanted more. Here were her arm follicles all groaning, giving off sound that matched the tone—the tone so omnipresent and gashed and slurping now that it had become a number on the air, pressed on all people. Her pores resembled tree bark, cracked and capped off with old lines of other age and rash and ranting, worn inside with where little bugs embarked, making new homes inside her fat, drawing strips along in rip to meld with other stations on the house. Here were the mother's tiny teeth—each one that much ouched over the other—screwing her gums deeper when they wanted—aching one another out—the nights of screeching—the endless bleeding—how she cared for them in floss—burned from white to orange to yellow, red to brown to black to gone—and yet here again, like doors. Here were the mother's birthing thighs nicked fat with sore spots grown wide as doorways, wide as suns. With the proper aim and angle and volition, one could lean into them and disappear.

I guess what happened then is the mother and the son, they walked, though there was nowhere for them to go. The grass where the neighborhood had once hosted a garden later used for ritual burial had grown so high it seemed a sea, and, surely, inside it, there were a billion bodies lost and rotting, as the stench that rose made wavy lines like heat grade on the hemisphere of breath. I guess the road that had always led out of the front gates to a street that led to shopping centers was now so cracked in so many places that the asphalt resembled undentisted teeth, the gaping mouth of all worn around them which would suck you in alive in stench.

The mother tried to lead her son into the manhole that hid the gutter from daily vision, down into the branching bastard yearlong labyrinth of pipe connecting all things elsewhere, though here the muck had washed up so thick it made a cake on top that you could stand on, through which in so many places on the surface you could see the reams of those who'd gotten stuck, their half-plunged bodies draped as if relaxing, sponged and nowhere, covered in machine grease and fleas.

Right.

So, the mother started one direction then another, turning, turning, aware of leaking gas behind her eyes—gas of nauseas, fear, contusion, gorgons, aping hate leashed in her teeth. She felt mammalian—*was she not?*—semi-destructive and in sudden want of death haunted by half-hung memories of glee—old warmth hidden in some kind of no longer present feeling. *Don't you feel ashamed?* something long beyond her kept repeating, and though she did not yet, she felt she did. Each hill surrounding seemed just to get steeper, each inhale came through a little less. In each place they went she called out for the father in the other name she could remember, no longer concerned by the Terms. She remembered the father's prior name and could feel it coming out of her pores and through her aspiration. She screamed the name without opening her mouth and in each place they went the father's name echoed and the walls or air of the places trembled by the gait of what had come out of her in light, and sometimes solid things were turned to liquid by her just by her being and liquid things were dried to sand, and the mother spun her head in circles looking through something wedged between her and her mind, the portholes lodged in the background of the flush of her skin, all inches of her begging in one long sound, *like the toning, but inverted*, and still the father did not appear.

In the light Person 811 found himself standing at the mirror shaving his face. He'd been there working the razor for several hours, he knew that. He carried the razor in his skin, where it had been gifted to him by his father, one of no number, who had pulled the blade out of the ground beneath them where they stood. For years the blade had sung for hours each night vibrating. 811 often felt it in his tongue or through his sternum. He'd run over the coarse skin so many times now there were mowed red indentations in his cheeks, strapped strips of almost bleeding where the flesh still sort of hung together. There was no more hair, and yet he shaved as if his arm did not belong to him.

811 had burst a woman once, by staring—the blood had spouted through her face—the curd had looped down from her nape and chest like gowns. Her body continued on inside the air that day and never came back. That night the father stayed out in the backyard practicing hypnosis.

The father had his own ideas regarding god.

The mirror, likewise, did not seem to hold him. In the cusp around his oddly glowing body there was a room he'd known before. He knew he knew the room but he could not say exactly why or what about it or who had been there once and when.

The room was blowing snow, or something else. A screen of light white powdered petals poured from the long flat ceiling onto the bed—matter that in other years had fallen on the father in other temperatures and locations and forms. 811 felt his body changing.

BLINK

There was a woman on the bed—the same woman he had seen before, from somewhere, though he could not decipher this, as her body had changed too: *her body less wrinkled in his presence than under any light.*

By her reflection in the mirror over his shaving shoulder, the father could see the woman mostly did not have a face. That is, she had a head and hair around it. The snow stuck in her hair. It did not melt into the hair, just clung there glinting.

The woman had a mouth of huge white teeth—this he could see. She had spent years caring for them, each, in full. But where the woman should have eyes and cheeks and nostrils, instead the father saw something else. Staggered beads of wretched colors, rolling in and on around against their texture like pixels flailing. Bits and pieces of other parts of other bodies, collaged. Bodies he had known or not known and did it matter. No, it did not matter.

The woman's face remained refracted as she lay there naked on the bed. She had a huge round ream of black film she used to wrap around her neck. She worked the film around her in a circle, passing hand to hand, the scream of adhesive whirring on over each inch of her body covering it gone. She'd already done her lower portions, her waist and arms and legs and tits and more—the woman's nipples were massive, 811 noticed, covering her whole tit mostly, black as a long and unlit hallway, slick. He still wanted to touch the tits, kiss around them, suckle—though by the time he felt that wanting in him all the nipple skin had been enmeshed. All she had left now not yet film-covered was her screwed head—the pulsing head of TV color—the slick blonde hair pulled to a comb—the father recognized this hair—he could smell it.

The woman's mouth was spewing coins—they gored in fountain down onto the mattress—all the metal money Person 811 had spent in years on other women, on his body, building size. The woman's cocooned body writhed among it, sucking the stink in. She, he recognized then, had been inside his home. *His home?* The phrase contorted in his flat mouth as he tried to speak it, spit it aloud. It wouldn't come out how he meant. He could not make the word alight upon the air around him. He felt the fat vein in his forehead squirt a little harder each time he tried—his larynx clucking with old smoke and dandruff—*the snow was dandruff*—the ceiling like some dead skin cracking in its still—the walls some celled portion of a larger thing—a thing that moved.

I still do not know… Person 811 said in someone else's voice. Still do not know… Still do not…

What the hell am I saying, he tried to say, and in trying could hear nothing but the tone.

The father found that he was not shaving now so much as laughing, rubbing an apple on his face. A chubby wretched apple, stuck with aphids. Its crumpled skin clung to his skin. He stopped and gnashed into the apple. He chewed the loamy gut, tasted hot hair oil and bleach. Inside his stomach he felt the pieces of the apple reconvening. He felt it stick in his throat width, holding certain words there. He had the razor in his hand again.

He began to shave his tongue—the tongue he'd used so many ways—the tongue that still would not form the words he wished. He tried to turn around and look upon the woman, *his young wife*, to bring some morning to this color, ask her to help him say the words right, ask her to tell him where and when and who he was, but still he could not make his body work. Instead he shaved—right to left and left to right, up and down and back against the grain, the bitter foaming cold cream itching where it clung and took the cells up, the hair and skin beneath him piling up in cold report.

The next time 811 felt himself allowed to look again the woman was not there. The room was not there. The space was gushing light. The light blicked in and out and off and on around him, against his chest and face. The walls inside him roared beyond.

He found that when the light was off he could move by his own will—his hands were freed, he discontinued shaving, he touched sorely smoothing sections on his chin—but in the light he could do nothing except see himself there with himself—another version of him across the room where the faceless woman on the bed had been. This double of the father was rather massive, more than in numbers. Its other body contained all of the room's space. It had eyes. In his own eyes enlarged before him he could see several people waiting. They spread their fingers on the flipside of the glass bulb of his eyes' lenses. Their fingers squeaked the eye with resin.

The other father did not blink. His enormous mouth opened and began spraying spittle and some stench—a crystalline wind that flapped 811's hair on his own smaller head and tucked his skin back. The skin was runny. The massive mouth was open—hot, a window, some new door—811 inhaled the exhale and felt it harden in his intestines. The lights kept blinking. The walls were neon-gravy colored. In the dark the father moved toward himself.

Back where the house had been the mother began to rebuild the house with what things she could find or make. There was not much there of the remaining materials around the home's indention that did not have the error of the tone all shattered in it, nor was the land right, and so she resorted to herself—to build the house out of the cells she'd carried in her blood and organs for this silent purpose through all those other years and other books. In the light around the gob of shit the house had stood upon and must stand upon again the ground groaned with a long low seam of all prior bodies' groans condensed.

The mother used a slab of rock to shear some of her skin off and this became the house's frame. The walls were thin and marbled and they wobbled on no breeze. The pockmarks or other frayed places on her size moaned wide and of a texture stung endlessly by wasps and poked by men and lathered over with chemicals aimed to keep her clean and calm her down inside the sighing night, becoming rooms and hallways on the air there. The mother spit into her hand and rubbed it hot and stroked it across clips of nothing to make windows, through which one could see out but not see in. She pressed them warm into the walls. She stood for sometime there outside in the reflection looking through it, believing each thing that might be needed into place.

Gaining pace now in burning sunlight, the mother forced herself to laugh. The sound became a bedroom, with air inside it she could breathe, and space to negotiate the catalogs of prior nights arranged in catalogs of deformed color representing…what? She could not remember. The forms were firm, though, and held mass. They buzzed around her body, waking sleep. The refracting air around the passing laughter became food, cells they would suck into their body in the mind of feeling pleasured, drawn with light. She plucked her wisdom teeth and fashioned clocks, each bent on counting every second gone here in the building held together, another she would never have again. She yanked her remaining hair out by the shallow roots and from these she made wires for the light, so that in the house she and the child could see each other coming, going. There would be places left to hide, places the light would not reach no matter how many devices the mother fashioned, any hour. From her eye she pulled a door, the front door that led into the house where here in coming days she would grow old with what was left of her by now. From gaps in her memory she made knobs with gears inside them that could turn to lock or to unlock. For keys to the keyholes she broke her index nails off, one for the child and one for her—she knew already if turned too hard they would break and there'd be no keys. The mother spoke into her hand and had each thing she needed. It was all right there, she found, if pulled in dark meat of her most tired parts.

The son paid no attention. His hair had grown out even more, enough to mask him from sun damage and from the buzzing remainder of the tone. He could not feel the button underneath his tongue—a button which, had it been pressed in at any minute, would have made the old house reappear in full, and they could have gone into the house in there and lived without a mind. All other days instead in simple presence of the unpressed button, consumed with all the other kinds of shit. He invoked himself in conversation, chucking long rocks at the unfinished Universal Roof, shouting for someone to come and touch his body, though at the mother's touch he balked. The worms were writhing in him also and in his hair he wore the dust of the collapsed house and the ground did not like him alive. He breathed and breathed it. He watched his mother work stuffing dirt and moss between the new home's walls of skin for insulation that would keep them warm or keep them cool, and would help to keep the sound there in or out around them, would pack them in and hold them nearer to each other.

When she was finished, cold and glowing, in the front door the mother carved their prior names, watched them sway away into the grain.

Inside the house it seemed the same house as the first one, the one the father had lived in alongside them there before, except for small facets such as the placement of light switches, hanging pictures. Some of the rooms had changed their shape from what a room is or seemed slightly off-sized in the day: a room shaped like a locket or a toothache or the waning of the moon.

As well, the air here was much colder—the mother's mouth made plumes that hung and stuck around her face, firm bots of breath she could reach up and grab hold of. Her exhaust formed shapes like little crystalline rooms again inside them, smaller copies of the shapes that held the other air inside the house around them. She put each shape to her ear and listened. Inside she heard someone speaking and another person speaking back. She tried to believe the things she understood them saying. She tried to want it too, and tried to tell it. She watched each shape one after another dissolve all dry and frying in her palms.

With each breath the mother took what she had made and set it on the ground, while the son, coming behind her, crushed the mother's breathing underneath his feet.

In the hall the mother found a calendar in which all the dates said the same day. On certain instances of that day someone had written things to do in what looked like her own hand:

JANUARY 1—CACKLE LESSONS
JANUARY 1—DON'T FORGET TO TURN THE CLOCK
JANUARY 1—HOLE DOCTOR APT., BRING KKKASSH!
JANUARY 1—WHO WAS AT THE WINDOW LAST NIGHT
JANUARY 1—WILL YOU QUIT EATING ALL THE CHALK
JANUARY 1—GOD THE WATER IS TOO HOT HERE
JANUARY 1—GROPE MOVIE
JANUARY 1—FILM YOURSELF STANDING ON A LADDER
JANUARY 1—CLIT PIERCING PROMISE
JANUARY 1—BRUNCH WITH GOD
JANUARY 1—LOOK BEHIND YOU

She ripped each page off as she read and ate it. She did not chew with teeth, but let her stomach have each unto itself, to swallow whole. A sheath of white bird feathers bloomed on her forearm and she brushed them loose with her thick nails. Her skin was watching.

I am getting tired of myself, the mother thought.

I am tired also, the son replied from a far room.

I am also very tired.

I would feel okay if you did not turn the page.

Why did you do that?

I told you I was tired.

You know how you and I are getting sicker.

I mean, it's hilarious.

We won't speak of this again.

In the new house the mother still found the door that held the stairwell, lodged like a razor in an apple. She had not built a stairwell for this new house, expressly. Someone was knocking on the door. The knocking made the whole house quiver like a fire. She touched the crack around the door. She traced its long shape with her knuckles. She felt a warmish crumbling kind of air there coming through. She felt the thing inside her eating. She felt her ribcage being toned on, nestled near to, giving birth to more of where she was again, every inch of her another child. She sneezed up a sofa and moved it over the door's face. She went to bed, though inside her sleep she saw the door again, and behind the door again another door and it was snowing something.

The father wriggled in the father. In the light he moved through corridors of chub, black spasmed pockets of hid body caught and aging. He did not know what about his moving was what moved him, only that when he nudged his head another way he would shudder from one crux to another, the air slurring into squirmy clouds of pinkish liquid, scent of want. He often thought he heard someone other coming toward him from the other way in the larger body, down the long blond hall inside him where he'd wormed. A strumming presence, something heavy like the name of cream and crushing putty on the air. He tried to hurry forward through him in the slather, kicking, barking, forming new minutes in his flesh. He found he could not at all remember which way he should be headed, which way already he had been or if he'd ever moved at all. Each inch had new tunnels, some so immensely black there was no way.

For each inch of the father there were many fathers. For each father in the father there was sound from which the body had been composed. The sound cased in around him making flesh. He couldn't see what his hands were doing. He couldn't see what his face was doing. Little worms caked in the walls around him were passing also through his skin and unto somewhere else. For years he'd swallowed pills to try to clear his system of its parasites and its ailment and none of it had worked, none of it had done anything except turn his shit a different color, which matched the walls of many houses and sometimes the color of his mind. The years still shaking in the father like the silence:

The year my final dentist fit his whole arm down inside me, hungry for a portal, high on light.

The year I would have been a husband to anyone here with my same eyes.

The year I said I thought I wanted more—and really did.

The year my fat shook itself free, became another body, on its own—one who would stand above me in the evenings, never touching.

These are not my years, the father tried to tell the years themselves inside his thinking, though the words his body thought were:

What else could I have loved.

Move! Person 811 heard himself outside himself repeating, this voice as big as he'd imagined something in the mind of some gone god's. Move, you massive dickless fucker!

He was already going fast as he could—the muscles in him stretched raw with windows in their gristle. He could no longer sense the other man following behind him, nor the man behind that man, so on.

All these fat, prismatic people.

The father breathed his blood.

Inside himself he felt the flesh walls to turn to water where he touched them—*because he was them*—a tasteless, scentless, flushing liquid that stung his lids and shrank his bowels. The other body all around him also seemed shrieking. In the color of it was the tone.

The father rolled along among the water folded and unfolding—grasping for the door—what door—some, any vision—a window—waking locations. He kept rolling. He felt several sections of himself go other ways, swimming in opposite directions at the same time, a separation in his skin. He could not think of which part of what to try to hold onto.

Above the water a black orb-camera kept panning back and back and back, capturing each blinking of the father in tunnel method of the smear. The face of the water was all placid seen from above it, despite the movement underneath. The camera ascended, its organs burning, until it hit some kind of perimeter or ceiling and was stopped.

The camera kept bashing at the surface, at the surface. It could not cause a crack in what held it there from moving further out. Something very warm beyond it seemed to murmur. The camera beat itself to bits, sending small fragments flying until it hit the vital cord and fell into the thing it meant to film.

The surface did not blink.

The father's body washed up in a bathtub. A nude woman stood beside it in the mirror working curls into her hair, long gray locks that ate the light up. She heard the father sputter, sneezing sea up, weed and scales screwed through his own hair. The woman had a long black metal chain that ran out from her vulva. The chain led somewhere beyond the bathroom door, its presence vibrating with a low tone. The woman continued with her fingers curling till her whole head was encased—her cheek skin slumped and slathered with bright white oil that clung to light underneath. Her tits, he saw, had been removed. In the tub, Person 811 burped and stammered, trying to stand up. The nude woman's neck was stacked with hickeys, kind of glowing. Her spinal column seemed disrupted. Her ass, though—her ass had spent endless time on glossy paper, replicated through the years. The father nodded. He felt his back arch, his fat toes cracking as they cricked.

The woman finished with her make-up and came to stand above him. The chain anchored inside her tremored taut—as if the chain itself or something huddled at the far end could sense her moving and did not want it—and yet the woman did not flinch—no emotion as the chain tugged up from her, peeling her skin in flaps up off the limb. Her eyes were hard and had no color. In the tub the woman knelt down on the father, pressing some fleshy wet spot on his gut. Somewhere downstairs animals were screaming, chipping at the walls.

The woman took the father by the dark balls and opened up her mouth.

WHAT'S THE MOST BEST THING YOU'VE EVER SEEN, she said loudly without speaking, her mouth full of his dick. WHAT'S THE ONE NAME YOU COULD KNOW WITHOUT KNOWING YOU KNEW IF YOU HAD TO WHO IS THE WAY YOU WERE THEN THERE WHEN YOU WERE THE WAY YOU WERE THEN THERE OR NOW HOW MUCH DO YOU LOVE YOUR HOME WHERE ARE YOU IN YOU

The woman's pores and eyes were gushing flour, some of which filled the father's nostrils and other holes, clogging his body to stay closed in. Cold spirals waddled up him.

When he did not reply, the woman shook her head and let the father's dick flop out soft against itself. Coming in contact with his other flesh now, the dick sort of sizzled and leaked liquid. 811 felt exquisite pain lurch up his sternum, ejaculating in the bath. Afterwards he still felt ugly. He watched the sperm worked through the water at his skin, searching through the mud there for some hold. He felt a billion others growing larger in his self-sacs, one for every sperm he'd not released. All of it squalling all inside him and around him bloating. And it burned.

The father opened his mouth again to try to say something to the woman, but she was older now; instead his mouth ejected reams of infant birds. The birds were slow and small and not like birds then, covered in a gel. They shat long white strings of old light as they flew up; they flew straight into the wall at once; they died. Their feathers fell upon his body, stuck against him, glued down with his ejaculate, still kind of strumming with future flew. They stuck too to the woman until he and she were under so much writhing neither could see where he or she began. Their muscles throttled in the mask. They shat so fast. The room began filling up with wet between the fiber, more gush and slick pushed from all their holes. *All ages fried.*

The woman's mouth said another question but Person 811 could not hear it through the gunk, the tone inside it making shriek. The beef inside him beating.

One massive hauling on the woman's chain inside the downy lather ripped the woman all of a sudden through the wall. Then it was dark. No matter how he struggled to flap and rise like what he'd seen come from her thereafter, he could not inside himself find hold.

The new men had to swim from several miles up, bleeding, to drag Person 811 out of where he lay, his body pussed and pulled apart and overflowing. The men had been employed. The men were not alive in certain senses. Where they'd lost their heads they'd been affixed with false heads made of leather, skin, and plastic, to give the appearance of having heads. The false heads bore great resemblance to Person 811.

Several sections of the father had become dislodged from the father in the toning, the elongation of his cells. The fleshy segments floated off among the liquid held to his body only now by bits of stringy flesh, vibrating with a language. The men collected these eruptions into a film sac—a bit of ear, a lash, a prism, something wet the father had swallowed years before—though some of the bit had washed out so far that they would not be found in time. The reconstruction of the father would therefore have to go on as best it could.

Underwater, the men lashed the father to a table and spun him upwards through the clear. They fit the father in a van. They drove the van into another van. This second van knew where to go. The van's driver had touched the father on the eye once, years before, in a gold room. The van's second-in-command had hid inside a blanket in the father's father's trunk for many months, breathing the same air as the father when the father's father drove him to and from the school. The father's father had never driven him anywhere but the school, and, well, once, to the ocean once to see where everyone they ever knew had drowned, to see the long intestines washing on the shoreline, and the massive birds growing more massive in their feeding.

The van's fuel had once been inside the father also, but not via the manner you might assume.

The van itself had once been used for rape, and would again, and would again.

Inside the van, Person 811 lay with his head down against the floorboards with the human moaning of the road.

In another kind of dark the men massaged the father's face. They stretched certain parts of him to yawning. They filled in the holes in with several kinds of putty and perfume orbs. The insides of Person 811 were now pastel. There men inserted devices in the father, items—*none of which by sight or function they could name*—inscribed text and digits on the father's cells and sperm and organs, grafted buttons—then the father was sewn up.

Person 811 was made to stand and laugh and say nice things, though his new tongue kept getting in the way.

When he could shake hands with satisfaction, the men took him to visit the naked woman's grave. She had perished in his pleasure, they explained. Pleasure had been administered, please recall. For your enjoyment. The enjoyment of the pleasure of it. The greatest light. Now if you don't mind:

sign this form. And this form. And spit up here. And as well here now make the creaming. Stamp, initial, spit up, making creaming, sign. Checks must made out to the Absorber. Keep your eyes open.

The men watched Person 811 kiss the ground. They watched him lick the woman's headstone and thank and thank it. Under the headstone was just putty. The woman had been absorbed or reassigned. Everything, they said, would be okay.

Okay? the father said. He could not taste it. Okay? Okay?

They pointed up.

They handed him a special pair of high-grade zoom bifocals that fit intensely to his whole face.

The word was written on the sky.

There in the weeks I came to know my wife again, the air was made of liquid ash

You could walk for weeks and step through windows and still just everything was old

Spumes of shit or wingbeat would come floating on some shudder

But for the most part, the house, the yard, in everybody—we knew black

We lanced around in squirmy currents cutting transitions for our hands

It wasn't funny, nor would it stop

In the ash you let your eyes and arms go and you would end up somewhere or another

You could just roll around and release shit

No one would know

Some nights I'd turn the a/c down or leave the fridge wide open and the black rooms would then turn harder, into ice

Then there'd be rungs that formed up in the transom

Then you could climb

I'd slunk through all of this alone

By the time I'd learned the manner of the ladder there was lather in the den

There were shapes among us and we could feel them

We could have them, or be had

I was raped in so many positions I can't remember by things I also can't remember

It felt like walking

Soon the long waves sunk off from the houses and on the air was left no light

From the dark rhythm I cut a woman's body

My wife of me was made of night at first, whereas I have only ever been all cold

Her voice would pour out of my skin asleep for hours

She had such undoing ideas

She had a talisman that gave off weather

There was so much between us we could touch and so much milk

Right now I can remember I am the father in this book

Right now, regardless, I remember, though soon again soon I will not

In this scum I'd built the house that would be ours

I built it just by blinking

It was right there

Just years and years and fucking years inside this house there counting

Moving in from room to room in no clean light

Often my wife was not around at all, or she was watching from somewhere I could not feel her

I could not feel anything

My skin would stick to certain surfaces for days and I would wait

Wait and ask and look and listen, peeling slowly, where I could

Watching the slow slim building of the soft house stacking forward up into the day

Once the current floor had flown up from me higher, I would not think of it again ever at all

Inside this house I could sleep as long as all I wanted

Which was almost always

My house to me only ever one flat level, as my father's had been

Inside the night, the air light compiling, the burst and lift, the sloping ground

The night we made the child along the air between us I'd been mostly overwhelmed

The air was crumbed and creamy and I'd been spinning with the scissors

You had to get at it from an angle to make the rooms things again that would not burst

I'd slipped up and racked my forehead three times

My wife was not concerned

She'd been talking to the rathole, where I swear I saw her forcing the best of all our food—the white pecans and goose hair

I swear she had it in for both of us

As I did too

I would tape her hands together for our sleeping but by midnight she'd chewed through

She took to knitting a parachute in case the world slurred sideways or inverted

There were so many things to come, she swore

My eyes by now were mostly swollen lids

I walked in the patterns I most remembered to our bedroom and rolled myself into the moth-made bed

For once I found the way to sleep by simply sleeping

I hid inside me in the world

I'd half cracked a dream of false condition—free fast food, water parks and mega-money—when I felt my wife's tongue in my cheek

It moved around inside me as if searching, as if after some compartment I had not found, the most mashed part of me stored white inside it, some lick I'd managed to keep mine

Her tongue touched my own tongue and made me speak a language I'd never heard

Those old tongues in me all full of other people

My wife there all above me in no light

We had been together for exactly fourteen days through all the banging

She ate my breath and held my hands

She let her tongue continue slit so far down deep into my throat I could feel it coming out the far end

I could feel it squeegee through my balls, the halls of ugly others of me all inside them, also speaking

Knowing all of our old names

It folded through me like a waking

Where I would go to be alone

Very soon our skins had changed

I heard the sound of metal drumming

The walls inside my sleep were slurred and pocked with goiters

There was a swan, a goose, a chicken—all of them pecking at my head from the inside—while on the out my wife would shriek and she was in me and I was in her—so

Then was someone other also too

My wife swelled up only from one point, her private center, while the rest of her curled dry

This was all within a matter of an hour

Her front became a thing against which I could lean

Then it became more than that

I could forget that I was there, though when I did this my wife would try to drink my body

My blood and such shit

The other of us wanted mass

Each inch had its own inches to derive and to comply to

My wife gave it all the rest that we had saved

She ate the ash that shook off from the ceiling

She made me go out into the yard and dig up a certain kind of nit—a thin translucent nit no bigger than an idea

The nit had a massive nest of eggs just like it, in its image, as were we now

My wife gave each one a little pet name before she slurped them through her sternum to the child

The nits replicated and came back out of her through where her holes were

As had I once been created, as had you

There were webs or nests all through the bedroom and beyond

This was all within a matter of an hour

One then another

My wife tried to hug me to her chest

I said Ouch a little, and she echoed it back at me

There were new lines in her eyelids and what beneath them

She was already unfolding

I felt my ribcage folding inward as the form inside her stomach kicked me in my own

She lashed and gnashed and shrieked up steam shaped like my face

I kept the door between us mostly always after

I slept with knives and mirrors and a bell

I heard her in the old rooms brimming over

I heard the child inside her coming out

There was a smell and some kind of gonging

I couldn't see, I closed my eyes

My body moved me through the house

I felt my each inch spreading out

There was more of me than I could need in any instant

There were more years then

There was the new edge of the night

Inside the house Person 2030 sat silent with his eyes closed scrawling drawings of himself. In each picture he'd made his gut appear enormous, like his mother's, filling up most any page—another person lodged inside him, like his mother. In some pictures the person was hair-covered, while in others it had no openings.

The child had made hundreds of copies of himself. Each one he named with longer numbers that weren't numbers. The paper filled the room. It caked around his face and made it hard to breathe. There was so much paper. The pages that appeared blank were fat with certain words where the child's sweat had kissed against it. His arms were throbbing. He could not stop drawing. His stomach in the pictures kept on growing and in his real stomach something moved—an odd shape shaking through his inseams, against his blood—he felt it stretch up along his body to his finger.

He bit his finger, sucked the foam. Among the mottled knots of flesh and tissue, there were a set of keys, a keyboard organ made of organ. The keys each had a different word imprinted on them. Each of the keys, when played, made the same sound. The child touched notes and felt his fingers burning. He felt the notes inside his head. For each note there were endless others at the same time in it bending what the note had meant to mean, and yet once played there was no way to unplay it.

Outside his shape, he heard the other sound, the shrieking of the tone, again beginning—*a tone*, he realized, *made of every sound he'd heard or uttered here so far and so too would utter then in years to come; these words that made him, in the book, and all the books read or dreamt of as they passed the words into the book of him in its creation.* He'd heard the tone many times before but never in a room here by himself. It struck the air so loud it shook his body to its strands—he could see straight through his skin—his skin now newly rashed in bumps that matched the pattern found on each of the bodies of him that he'd drawn, and too the bodies in the bodies growing, written in their 2D lard. He moved through the room's light toward the sound. At first it seemed to come from one direction then it spread out into spirals. In the spirals the child moved. He wobbled through the kitchen to the hallway where down the hall he saw the door.

He had been told not to touch this door. *The door would burn him*, the mother warned in her sleeping. *The door would eat your mind. It is terrified of everything.* Along the hall the child bonged back and forth between parallel walls. He shook inside himself where the blood inside him bonged along also. There were pictures on the walls of earth from far away and overhead but he elected not to see.

The door had not a knob now but this did not stop him from making it come open.

Behind the door he saw the private stairwell where his mother once with another man had hid, though now instead of down the stairs went up.

Each stair had a unique symbol traced in dark epoxy.

The child could not quite see as he ascended. He could not see the frame of the house or its condition or the way the space around him stayed one size as he moved forward on its air. The stairwell seemed much thinner than it should be in some places, so thin that the son had to turn profile and scrunch against his side, dragging himself upward using his convulsive muscles to draw himself along the banister in shifts. Sometimes the stairs became automatic and the son could hold on and ride clean.

At various points along the incline the stairwell opened into rooms. The child came upon a room swarmed with tiny flies. They were coursing over objects, like a long land. He moved into them full, regardless, as if he knew why they were there. He recognized the patterns in the layers of them. He listened to them breathe. They caked around the son's face until there was no face left, sucking, until the insides of the son flowed dry. Then all again he was ascending, stairs beneath him. His ass and legs already burned.

The markings of each stair's face burned low with an old glow, each feeding some form of murmuration through his legs. The son had no reason to go on upward but he knew he could not go down—there was no remainder of the stairs that had brought him to this level—and with each step the well behind him disappeared.

Further on the stairwell opened onto a large and long white building, higher than he could crane his head to see to look. The building had thick curtains closed and glowing in each window, silhouettes. He could not find an entrance into the building. He pressed against it. He moved his hands all through it as through milk. Someone was reaching on the far side for him, then he was falling. Then he was ascending again on the stairs, and soon another landing opened down into a house, into a room like the child's mother's bedroom had been as a child herself.

She was there sleeping. She seemed the same age as the son now. Her hair was long and clean and blonde. Her eyes were open as she slept. She watched the son move there above her. He tried to speak and he could not. Through the walls a screeching filled the old air, like the prior tone but backwards, as if captured in his blood. The girl smiled. Above the bed he touched his mother's face with his face and together they drew air and then again the son was no longer in the room there but still ascending and wished he wasn't but he was. There were so rooms many the son could not remember each, one after the other. On each the son could not remember how he kept finding his way back to the stairs. There was always more blank space and further eras.

Some levels up, in ripping heat, the dark stitched so thick that it was liquid. The child crept along the frame contorting. The texture of the walls along the stairs felt like a person but it had no color and no sound. He continued on until he felt one of the steps go flat beneath him and the floor spread out into a panel on which he could move further in one direction. The meat of his feet screeched underneath his other layers. A certain length into the space he felt his leg muscles going weak, bowing his stride out in long elastic loops. His bones inside him held the tone. Slow fur grew and subsided on the son's dry inches, making rasp sounds at his teeth, alive.

Further out the floor's face seemed to soften—his feet sunk in as if at flesh. He could no longer locate where the stairs had been behind him. He continued into the brim-mouth gaping, sinking further and further in— something stuck sucking at his eyeholes—corrosive pressure bloomed in bolts, stretching and aching at the flesh around his nostrils, between his teeth. There was a slur then—it welled around him—he could not stop going and he could turn away—he could not blink or cry out in help or warning as there was no word in his blood. Vast stinking suction pulled in against him, stretching his face into a mask that had no edge and gave off smoke. He felt the ball-bulb's pupils pop one after another, screeching holes that warm nails fit in. Micelight spread into his skull with pissy gold. The gouge sunk nausea through him like a yo-yo— it recoiled into his throat—made his tongue harder—bowing his stomach and the small black sacs surrounding.

He fought to stand. His back cracked in cartoon screwing. He began to cough a white wide light, a light that cut the son inside him as it sparkled through his gut to course the room where as the tingling settled in his shoulders, he saw among the heavy glow how all the space was stuffed with sleeping people, their mottled bodies packed in naked, flesh to flesh conformed and still conforming. Many of them had no faces. Many others had no heads. Even those that did seemed to blur where they were built, their features changing in floods of color and old mud. The room around them also glistened. There were no girders, no corral bins of the walls— only the mass of bodies comprising distance and nearness. The proximity of their tight-knit skins held each other upright and unconscious, writhing in REM. Their eyeseams stung crusted with yellow sleep shit and their veins twitching in their lids and arms and necks. Some of the heads spoke aloud into the air above them, a language shattered, throttling the room. Some of the bodies tried to walk or hide in fear of the child's entrance, pushing themselves against their neighbor, so crammed their skin owned bright red lines of indentation where they bent. Most seemed not to sense the son at all. They were old or not, and strong or not, and rich or not, and they had every color eye and face and blood. They wore the faces they only wore when they felt that no one could see them. The son could not tell at either end where the splay of bodies ended and the house again began. Their fleshy ocean stretched far back to no edge, except up to the border where he stood, his own unopened blood still gushing from his sockets to his hands. He felt the air inside him growing fatter, sticking to where he was there, his body brimming out around his eyes. He could not see clearly, then less clearly. He could not stop it. He felt him open up his mouth and he conformed.

The child spent the next 37 years again stunned in an oblivion while around him in the house the house stayed still.

When he could see again the room was bound, stuffed full of tape. Black film had wrapped around the contents of whatever had filled the air before it, glistening cocoons of several sizes. All terror buildings and bridges and the forests in the same folds. There were several kinds of silent light. All of the light was dark too at the same time. You could see the shape of day as if engraved. The light gyrated from the center of the room, light made of liquid, light made of skin, light made of light that could not hold itself together, and all around the land laid long in all directions flat and scrawled against itself, black but visible to beyond perimeter by the failing of the eye. The child could hear the sound of huge projectors. He began to move and could not move. He was standing hard against a warm thing, a thickened surface, some kind of screen. The pixels of the screen bent where he touched them, harboring the land. He went in the dark to turn around. The walls were nearer now than ever. The room the child was in was the same size as the child was. The land went on and on. He beat and banged against the glass and called her number. He called his number and nothing changed.

He held his breath and closed his eyes. He found that not breathing felt the same as breathing. He found that through his lids he could still see the same walls in the same room, though in the room now, held inside him, the screen no longer showed all endless lands, but instead now was reflective. The child could see only himself, though it was not like looking on into reflection. When the child moved his arm the other of him did not move. The other of him was much older and was naked and had no head. The man's arms were swollen where his were childish, the skin all covered in tattoos, each glyph distorted into shapes indistinguishable for what they'd been sometime or ever, the shapes of continents submerged. The child could see straight through the thin pale skin stretched on the man's chest. All through his organs small things had nested, thousands of them, *innumerable white birds*. The child could the muscled veinwork crinkling in the birds' sternums, their tiny marbled spinning eyes. The child began to raise his arms toward the surface and instead the man was moving his older arms, and then the arms were all around him, forming an oval, or a hole. The room's film wrapped around the child's face and the man's face and their fingers and their chests, around their torso and their middles and their leg meat and down their mouths all through their bifurcating encased holes. The edge of the film slit the child's and the man's esophagus and trachea, wrapped over organs. Their blood was pouring back and forth all between blood. The child could feel a voice performing through him, moving his tongue too so that he too said the words, not numbers or names now but other symbols, the language written in the book he'd always thought had been only a mirror.

The child found himself again inside the house. He was standing in a small room without windows or decorations or furniture or paint. The room was hardly larger there than he was. A sound all knotted in his face. He felt his face and it felt older. There was nothing to look into. The room around him was all language: where there meant to be a chair he just saw *chair*. When he looked down at where he felt his arms were, he saw nothing.

The child moved back out of the room. He saw it was the door to where before he'd found the stairwell. There were no stairs there. The air felt calm. The child looked at his arms and felt they seemed the same as any hour. He closed the door to the room and locked the door with his long nail.

The milk of air was winding through the house. It knew the house and wanted through it. It wanted to fill the air of the house and filled the space of the house's shape itself. Milk all through the years in lather leather held out only by an idea.

The child came into Person 1180's bedroom. He moved to stand above her bed. The mother's face and hair were crusted white. Her cheeks had marks of small incision. The child cracked his knuckles with no sound and watched his mother's body shake. He could not remember her in younger form, the air among them then, the light of the rooms contained, the many buried spheres of dark all gathered in his linings.

Through the sheets and through the mother's gown and through her stomach flesh he could see the flesh all building in her, spreading the space of where it was into the room around them filled with her or someone else. The liquids in her knitting where she wanted and was wanted. The fields inside her silent. He leaned against her. He pressed against her. The sound he'd carried in him from the room of the younger mother changed—turned on its side inside him, pinking the edges of a color captured in the sound hid in the flesh, the ancient color between colors slaved and waving.

In the room around the child, the walls began to pour, a liquid leaking from the holes the house had all throughout it onto the air the house contained away from other light. Some of the gush turned into eggs or maggots, sometimes to birds, which flew up and at or into the son's head, squawking, clawing at his eyes. He tried to shout the mother's name but instead everything else kept coming out—a shattering sound the son had only ever heard inside him in there eating at the inside of his face.

Soon it was impossible to tell where the walls ended and floor began, or where the inside met the daylight, where any of these surfaces ended or began, or where the sky above it all claiming the buildings separated them from that, and whatever lay beyond it. Outside the house the ground was skin and ash. All of the surfaces were slurring. The substance pooled around his flesh, its color coming from his holes and joining with it. His new skin stuck to the air. The color covered up his face and arms, the light surrounding. It was above him, and beside him, folding over where he was, though from outside himself he just seemed standing, staring, in a room. It seemed any day becoming. He thought to raise his arms and watched them raise. With the cells grown out each suddenly long as both his arms on every finger he clawed and clawed at the wet but found it felt just like any air and nothing changed.

Outside the house inside the sound again there coming off it the remaining men mashed sky to skin. It had been ages as the day broke. The space of each body near and nearer at each other in the revolving stroboscopic sudden air all wet with an interlocking hum of digits gripping fast at what they passed, each instant ripped from that one prior, an old dry fire buried in the air. The men could not quite find their way to fit into the house now—the cells kept mixing. The night was crushing. They seemed already in the house. The length of rooms wobbled around them. From all the windows there was mass.

Around the house for miles the bodies swarmed stuck against it—men conglomerating men, men but not men but bodies full all of men and women only ever, eggs and knotting throttling their flesh. One by one the mass grew larger, hoarding skin sacs pillowed whole. The bodies were strung with muscle, crick and crap redoubled, packed in damaged intestines and flat minds. A massive bulge somewhere goaded on the distance small and sweltered, a gift sent in the guise of sickly rain, beating the house's seams in waves as had the waters. All gave knocking. There came all knocking in and on around the house and pounding rounder, toward zero. The knocking flickered the lights in every room—it caused all adornment from the walls where walls were never wanted—the paint in sheaths rotting through hues, the pictures crumpled beyond image, the curtains scorched to gowns of ash, bright fibers wriggling where nothing held—it spread all through the soil and pilled it under, inward, crumpling the land and calling out.

The bodies swam and spread in and over one another, pushed inside their common flesh. They were nearly all one body throbbing, a cortex spread and slurred upon the day in heat. The body had so many mouths and eyes and ear holes—there was so much they could take in—their nostrils sniffing up what they could force, their fingers wriggling for some hole. Their pressure piled up around the house and rutted at their skin strips coming open. A hulking heat pooled up on certain scalps, scorching the hair off of their arms. All of their voices stuttered out at once, counting aloud, each human want they chewed through, *One one-thousand, two.*

For years the father walked in darkness. There was nothing about the way. The field was low and flat and he could not see it. No matter how far or fast or which way in the dark he moved it was the dark.

The father ate the sweat off of his hands. In his mind he imaged catalogs of food he'd eaten all the years in all the other rooms and he ate them all again. Once he had eaten the food out of his mind it was no longer there and could not be eaten any further, though it was stored in rungs hid in his fat. The father felt the fattest he had ever. The fat was all around him.

Through the darkness, fat made sound. At first from far away it sounded like the tone did—pearly and piercing, bone on bone pummeling skull— though as he grew closer in wherever it was familiar music, even if he could remember why or how. It colonized the light it, made it layered, layered the layers, split them wide.

The father followed the sound for further years again inside the same space until he was standing at a screen. The screen was silver, comprised of private light. The light was wider than his arms, wider than the space of wet he'd been contained in, and than the container of that wet, and that beyond. He went to move inside the space to touch the silver and found his arms were stuck hard in his sleeves. He could not move. The room fit down around him, sucking his cells. He closed his eyes and saw the silver shudder. There were ten of him, then even more. There were more of him before him in the silver than he could count, each of them more like him to him than he was himself. They had bodies he remembered being, arms and faces. Even when they did not resemble him exactly he understood. The bodies were all around him touching. They were talking. It was so all at once there was no inch. It felt like sleeping. He went again to open up his eyes.

The room was dark. There were walls there, stairs beneath them lit with ovals. He could move now, but only downward, as where before there'd been the screen there was what seemed by touch to be a ceiling but in fact was just the sky.

The father continued down the stairwell in the dark until he found a door. It was black and locked and had no number. The space behind the door was sort of humming.

He leaned and spoke into the keyhole. He said Hello, I am the father. His voice felt weird, somewhat like him but quite much thicker, cracking at the edges. As he said the words he felt them leave, sucked again into no sound. His head was wet and cheeks and ass were wet and holes were wet and he seemed shrunken. He touched his jaw as if to make it go again. His touching fleshes gave off sparks that gave him words.

The man said I am sorry I could not remember but now I remember many things I think and as time progresses I will continue to remember more things and there will be more things to remember.

I have been only here forever.

I will know what I was meant to be.

The door would not open. He pulled and pulled it. He called and begged and called the names and tried again. He pulled at the door and banged at the door and shook himself against the face of the door unchanging until there was nothing left about his fingers or his hands.

He turned around and found the world.

Inside the house the small door to the stairwell opened and a man came in. He could not remember what had just happened in the body of the father. In the hall the air was wet. There was so much heat there, like a furnace, though there was no one in the room. The walls were running thinly with clear liquid that made it glint wide with the light. There was no mother and no child. There was no noise of people or the men there and through the window the day was calm.

In the light the man seemed clean. He had been upholstered with new skin and hair. He had a smile that stretched the corners of his faces into small abscesses in which mud and rot had took to clinging.

If the version of the house built by the mother from her body had held a picture of the man we know as Person 811 in it somewhere, which it didn't, this man standing in the front hallway, he would look nothing like that other man. Some would say, then, these two could not be the same person. Some would say this discrepancy inside a story could cause a problem. Like how one would expect two cars driving at one another from in opposing direction on the same straight road to be piloted by different drivers. Another idea to consider is how when a furnace turns itself on in a house, whether there is someone home or not, there is a clicking sound and there's a glint.

This man who seemed to have to be the father, Person 811, *whoever else*, despite the problem in his appearance, he couldn't even spell his current thought, though he had it tattooed on his knuckles, between his teeth. He tried to walk along the hallway. He had his arms steadied out beside him as if learning. He was saying something he couldn't make come out quite right. The words seemed strung inside his mouth and blinking as if some rheumy cord of Christmas lights, his eyes slightly bulging from his head in bulbs of water. His feet left puddles on the carpet, puddles in which no reflection of the air around him shone. The man waddled past the small door that led into the kitchen and continued onto straight to the wall. He banged his skull and heard no sound.

At the wall—where before there'd been a space to go into the house, for all those years—he went on walking heavy with his forehead pressed flat and firm into the fiber. The new wall was affixed with a mirror, same as the one he remembered from another room aged in his life, though never before here. The man looked head on into his own face, the other of him there embedded. He looked at the symbols of the language burned on his skin and flexed his muscles. He did not remember having ever worn the clothes in the reflection—a black shawl, a wire bib, blood down his arms—or having worn clothes at all ever for that matter. He touched his reflection's face and then his face. He put his thumb into his mouth to taste the thumbprint and see if it could matched the pattern of his gums. He looked into the man's eyes and the man looked back.

Their shared expression was one like hope.

The man spent the evenings with his ear against the house, feeling with fingers in the ridges that there would be something to draw in and hold near. This is not what he'd expected. This was not the color of the carpet. This was not his head growing all this hair. There was so much moving in there among the insulation, and yet he had darker color in his eyes. He the mother's mistakes and misgivings in their home's creation down scribed in long illegible music down in his arms. The notes read one way on the paper, and another way when spoke aloud. The reading made his hair grow long. There was so much the man wanted to shout aloud into the house after whoever, but something in him ate the language out of his mouth before he could ever have it go, or other times the words would get caught behind his eyes and shoot off guns there, black cracking igloos of birth pellets. He could feel them in there bugging, lapping the lens curve, gagging up.

He wanted to walk some way into the room where the living room had been—where he'd sat nights beside the mother with TV light around them—where he'd eaten so many meals when there were meals to eat, microwaved or mashed and slathered—where there'd been pictures hung of him with others, laughing, touching, held in time—if he could just feel that again, a little—though no matter where he went inside the house and all the rooms about it and around it or what the rooms resembled, he could not find that room. He kept feeling the room he needed would be the next room in the sequence, but each time the next room was a room he'd already been in remade, a room he did not recognize in this condition, or there would just be wall and then more wall. The man felt something was pulling him away from the place he knew he needed to be going and back toward another room inside the house.

He tried several times to go back to where the door he'd come into the house through had been—the stairwell unto floors unending—though where it had been before it now seemed not—only the continuing flat surface of where the house was, holding what beyond him there all out. It was as if the door had never actually been there—as if it were a door existing only ever somewhere in his mind meat, burbling with knots.

Holy fuck someone is attacking my goddamned mind, he tried to say, but the words were fat and clung inside him. The words were bigger than his heart, his head, the house, and all of it was creaking.

The man was growing old already in this new place. He felt the rinds rolling through his leg joints, his muscle eaten up with acid called ideas. He looked already older than he'd even imagined he could ever, older even than his own father if his father were still alive now and if he remembered that man at all, though inside him he seemed growing younger, scrunching in his skin's cold shell. No time seemed to pass from one room to the next room or however long he waited for the words.

Let me live forever there inside you please god, the space inside him seemed to be saying, though he himself could not make the voice come out.

Let me eat.

Inside the house alone regardless the man moved what furniture was here now back to how it seemed that he remembered it had been, or would have been had it been in the house before. He wasn't sure why he felt he knew that but it was in him. He tried to make himself at home. He used his spit to wax the wooden seats and sofa arms more to his color—the house had lost his smell. He spread his sneeze and urine around the room in handfuls, along long blank walls he could not find his way behind. The walls would shake and break before him but still be walls there. No room could keep him long enough to be. The air made lesions on his teeth and traced the spaces in him where he wanted silence. He drew a small round square in the center of the room with more of his blackened, leaking blood where he remembered once there'd been a rug, where on other older nights the father would have liked now to take a coffee and watch men on TV throw themselves at one another for the bliss of many thousands screaming, shaking air.

Another TV in his skull turned on and off, each screen when lighted showing scenes here previously described, though with the father holding all the roles of all the people there combined, each way when dark again he could not feel the air at all around him.

The dicing day began to lean. Through sudden holes there in the walls around him, the man heard what somewhere sounded like the sound inside him recorded as the mother's moan, so many voices baked in one sound, but he could not really recognize the sound or what it was and when he moved through rooms to where he felt sure he'd heard it come from, it was not there. Windows would look out onto the house held there again, another house with people in it too blurred to turn toward him. Colors of a shaft or panel would split when he stare. The grade would spit up in his face and make his face spin, though once it calmed he felt thereafter also calmer, thicker, nice. He rubbed his glands and braced his eyes, *time catching time there where time had meant to never be.*

The space in this house where there should have been the mother's room had no door here on the hall, and yet the man stood in the space where it would have been not even knowing and touched the wall and looked at it and touched his face again and thought about the wall and what behind it and touched the wall again and waited and could sense something but did not know what or why or why this wall or why the other doors were disappeared and what he would have wished that he would find there waiting for him behind a door here if there were one and he could have it. He punched his muscles with his fists until both were bleeding and with his blood on one of the small walls he traced another door. The door did not have any number, no crease around it, but still it was a door.

And he kissed the door and kissed the door and kissed the door there—felt it move around his face like milk.

The man came into the room and stood above the woman in the image of his wife. He did not recognize her—her skin had shifted texture, kind, and size. There were no walls there where there'd always been walls there around the bed where they had slept and breathed and spoken in the night unknowing. There was no time inside the way. The father watched the woman sleep and breathe without clear rhythm. There was something thrilling in her pose—the way her hair encaged around her head stung on the static of the small room's excess electric charge—how even from here, through lengths of air and glass, he could smell the smell of him about her, the smell of her on him. She was shaking.

In something about the air between him and the body of the woman, the man could taste the grain each time he breathed, the rush of which itched all through his lungs and pelvis as if accelerating his body's aging even in spite of the slender or uncertain and translucent screens that in his memory the state said to have erected around each and every neat locale, and were claimed to have caught the brunt of the crap and cancers and what all else some god had dreamed to wear their lives—the state's voice the only clear one through and through him, ordering his veins, though at the same time scored on all sides by the tone beyond it, shaking in his sight.

The man tried to move toward the woman and found that he could not—he banged his face hard on the instant. There was a field there struck between them, not all unlike the mirror glass or any window framing day, though at once thicker and thinner, wider and nearer, there all at once and not at all there, *black beyond black*. Behind the cell the colors of the woman in her layers layered through him and sunned into him and struck the sound out of his eyes. He could remember things they'd done and said together, where they'd been together, what they'd been together, though he could still not remember who she was. He had no phrase for it and did not want to.

The man kicked and licked the surface there between him and the woman. Why could he not just touch her. He wanted to touch her, not just in the way he'd always known, but in something else about him. The glass persisted. The room's walls were even less there in the bedroom. He watched the liquid from her purr. The sound all in his ears from her and all surrounding shook colors from him too, turning his skin a glassy color to match where he could not move him holding hard. He knew the surface knew what it had to hide. He knew it knew he knew there was something there between them, something the man had had once, a view.

The man barked. He peeled a pretend sun down. He comprised his hand into a fist fumbling to keep the fingers flexed—there was something about them they did not want to bargain on—no curling center—he beat himself against the seed. He beat until something in him made the silence other, began to turn it. Beneath the flesh he could see where his cragging purple fodder pooled—purple not purple but sixty kind of color, and from each another wash of each—*god, the last time he'd cut himself it stunk so much*—his mouth came open all around him—his legs around him—his body made among itself and among her, grasping his breath in reins and clawing for cover—small as all the rings on all the fingers. His head against the silent space felt cooler, flatter, like a surface formed to fit into crevice bent to hold his shape—*yes*—he felt her body press against him—he felt the breathing—he felt a murmur in the earth—there was no tone then—*I could not count it*—fire barking through the fits of going on—with each day so short and nothing in it, it would not matter how quick the cooling came.

In a den of water well beneath them, an oil-thick sea far underground, the amalgamated film spools of the father began ejecting from a small hole in the sand. The film spooled out into the waters, amassing around the spigot in a cloud. The images in replicate kissed in wetness, melding—frames banging into frames—lacing through other older frames of other men and women already held there—*any person*—black hours slithered through a common liquid, finite years. Fish and bacteria nipped at the celluloid and chewed some of it out, relaying bits of frame into the waters, thrumming with them into foam and lather, subdividing the wet night. In this way the endless film spread along the long floor of ocean, rising up and out and on, while far above, there on the surface, the other men were growing mold, light in their eyes, moving in the same motion the mouth set in the man's own head vibrating and peeling at the edges of the transparent.

The mother found that she was walking. What was all else had disappeared. She could not remember how long she'd been asleep or ever sleeping. She was not in the house as she remembered making, but a long wide surface like the outside, countless edgeless corridors and pockets white as paper, yet contained. The room's comb wore a crusting curtain through which another nothing glowed. Her blood slushed on the air around her, built a lather on the floor. The mother could no longer think of what number had been her name for so long, or that she'd had one even then. Each time she tried to think at all she was just walking.

At the end of the hall the mother found the hall opened up into a room shaped like an orb. The room loomed huge and was not like any room come into before in any home. She could see a long way over, on the other side, a door that led into the room that had once been the room the hall led into. She could see a lot of something shining, so much it turned her eyes another shade.

The blank before her held an old sound—the room so wide and pink, squirming with metal. There were little nodules on the ground, emitting more. The nodules tripped her, in slow motion. When she fell, their vibrations caught and kissed her face. Through the nodules she could see into the house as from above. Smoke wrote itself in code over the mud surrounding. Old windows purpled cogging in the light. Inside, she and the child and the father there inside one room, making their day there, all days engorged into one scrunch, so thickly built in gathered action they were not moving. There forms each sat together, holding still, frozen through all the motions there enacted, the air around their faces all a blur. She could not tell what they were doing and did not need to.

She stood again and again and walked and felt the room expand. With each step her organs juggled just a little, ridged and glowing, making room for something else. The tone vibrated through her body. The more she moved the louder that it grew. She kept her eyes ahead. She did not flinch among the weird spray as her blood wrote itself across the air.

BLINK

The mother's blood formed endless stairs.

The stairs aimed downward, though this kind of downward at the same time was also up, and also was straight forward or backward on any given air, and also never moved at all.

The stairs seemed to never have an end.

The mother found that walking on the stairs felt no different than just breathing, doing nothing. She kept walking, falling forward, taking each stair among the sudden claps of massive light.

The mother felt certain, any stair now, she'd recognize a place she'd been—a room where she had lived once, somewhere to sit.

The knives and blades of every instant unremembered gleaming all around her cut her body, burned her eyes.

The cities waiting to be given.

BLINK

In the sheen of blood there somewhere far down, somewhere way below the house, below the ocean under these houses no one in this book had ever found—a black wet large as silent ideas, piled together in tiny other orbs lathered in bruising juice—the mother touched the first end of the film of all their years in all their minds—hers and the father's and the child's—each of the many men—each of the inches of the house. She looked into the frames and saw her many versions, the fray of the earth set in the warped celluloid—she saw the slush of those gone bodies, their screech and stutter, speaking all through her with one word, a sound like the tone through all the days there at once, all the words inside them, vibrating her lips. She inhaled the word where she'd just thought it and felt it spin in her again and come back out, its digits blurring in her colors.

She fed the flat end of the film into her mouth. She could taste the emulsion and the shade of each frame going through her. She ate each frame slick and small, the film there threading in her blood and organs. She chewed until her jaw hurt, then she sucked. Then she was only ever drinking, then only breathing, being, then just nothing. The film showed through her skin. The space around began to lean and change its color. Her form stroked phrases on the air. It spoke in code and complex whining that made the skin along her forehead eject jewels she'd swallowed in the night—jewels from necklaces and rings she'd worn in other rooms for occasions and ceremonies, the endless people, *some of which she could recall*. The numbers all bled together. 1, 6, 15, 28, 45, 66, 91, 120, 153… *No*. The presence made the ceiling above her shape turn translucent, but with such strained eyes even inside her she could not see. She was getting stronger through and through in old milk, though not enough yet to crush the crystal screeching in her gums.

BLINK

BLINK

The mother's shape was turning inverse. She was so wide now she could not stand up on her own—and yet the presence's long voice made the hair on her cheeks and forehead quiver. Her tendons stung so strained under duress that she would wobble horizontal in sick dance, the wall weight shaking song out of her mouth. 190, 231, 276, 325... finite, unending— each fluted inch producing many new, and each new inch producing also in the midst of its production other inches and thereon—her and the wider lining stretched inside—her throat swelled up with cells like little hallways, bedrooms, pockets waiting to be filled. The mother's glands grew larger than her head, the mother's head itself hung fat, encrusted, lined and bloating through its space and space surrounding speaking. Her flesh pocketed with nests. Tiny winged things snurted from the mother's mouth and packing in along the walls—eggs giving birth again, again, again, eggs giving birth to eggs—each as before imprinted with a language she could now somewhat in some way read, the barf of phrase and shit of sound strumming her slick with old orgasm, erupting tunnels—the flesh around her eyes hiding her eyes. Her backbone crimped till she bent up and over, back between her flabby curtained gut, all the way around, around, around in spiral until she'd knotted to a dot. Against her mind the space of days touched submerged again along the fruit rash of her labia and blouse, her years there held inside her wanting all other years back. For lengths she seemed to be floating on an ocean of old sweat and acid, her stomach full not of this ruined presence, but more light. There were so many other of her crushed upon the air there—husks of her she'd hid or lost to smear or deformation—the mother with mouth froze open and fingers crossed behind her back and knuckles riddled with so many rings they were not so much fingers as spiny, metal, gleaming knobs—the mother mushed in old mold from one she'd buried deep the longest, the one with the fleshy spirals hid up beneath her bitten nails, flesh all riddled with tattoos, a catalog indexed names and dates and numbers, textures beyond touch. Their colors gored all through the feeding prisms turning off and on again in strobe clotting the walls inside the sound. The house would reappear around her shape in clicks and patches, gone slightly longer every instance. The birds and eggs in nests in each of her there lathered over, crushing each other in the soft devices rolled, the color trapped in her sockets, an old flesh rising.

BLINK

She passed through seasons. Through the living. She passed through decades framed in gauze and water rising through long flat black packets held just beyond the edge of sea all slick and black, steam rising from it in a cold breeze as children dug their knees into the sand along the lip of water and let it lap the cells off of their arm, laying the layers against the ridges in the weight, while far beyond the water, under shrieking sunlight, clusters of white buildings without doors or windows rose high and thick into the sky so tall among the waters they could not be told from where they pierced whatever and continued on beyond all vision.

BLINK

Inside the wet, her body blinked and blinked. Behind her lids the years were strobing—she spoke their image on the air—they made more white surround them—they burned it open. With each syllable spent uttered, her body grew another creaming yard—yards of lash and lung all overflowing. The birds becoming hyper-larger from her too, feeding off her body of the cells choked down into them through their bird veins in what maze, and shitting right back out into the house's walls in symbols pooling ageless from her whole: …this bloat opening inside me… this whole width of my mind's need… these… these… these folding floors…

Outside the house it roared a dry white lather. It rained down rubber horizons, wide floors of paper, bags of cold. A wider section of the air glowed in small eruptions, mirrored leanings, half-hung burn. The earth went beat with hammers in the lungs. Liquid forms coating the lengths of what had been where hours uttered, covered over in the shaking of themselves. I mean the day inverted, as it could not have. Every inch filled with itself. Dirt rubbed its holes and called for filling in where it had been filled in already and filled again until the sound enslaved its sound. Rocks expulsed some human wish, as if in them, in their dark flat flesh, there was someone who once had held a tongue inside another. For certain lengths that house would fade. Prismatic mechanisms lurched on through the long dark, made of sleek metal, no lights, no pilots, scanning the nothing for the same. The rip of sky went on unfolding, the sky's clipped segments made to lisp. On the air behind there'd stay a residue of the sound and dust the house had held all naming nothing.

The sun beat the spit out of all else, bare. The scored face of the weird land around the house now in the light was scored, nattered with insects of pixels scratched from their encasements, shook off the foundation's creaming seams. In blue hordes the sound of the enmassed men crawled upon the long smear of the folding ground where the house disappeared and reappeared, rotating through the order all surrounded with what bodies full of sick sound noise and vomit, aching blistered, bumpy, long. The sludge was full of men and they were full of sludge. For each word we'd ever spoke the tone came on and on again around where we had been or never been.

BLINK

The sound of glass bowing and swimming up in shapes conditioned moments stretched by hands and putty. Sound of splinter and of long light and of the walls becoming throttled, bending in—the resin sledding off the ceiling, where for years their breath and speech in layers had collected in cold cells.

BLINK

BLINK

The sound shook the son and father in the same room, inches apart in different air, folded over face to face in variation. Each turned their heads as if to see and seeing nothing, they continued turning, their bodies corkscrewed with their flattened heads. As they turned back together, at the same time, they could not see there where the other had just been—some softened walls where the house's split clear between them, though the rooms seemed the same size. The son could hear the way the house was ripping, its room rubbed against one another in quick friction, birthing bolts of brown steam up from the carpet, tiny knobs. Through matching holes burst in the several ceilings up above him, he could see outside an upward awning spreading open over all—some off, charcoaled color. He felt the awning also rushing in him, pushing at his organs, on his teeth. He could feel his arms all stretched and draping as his colors fled to change.

BLINK

BLINK

BLINK

BLINK

A revolving architecture, wallowed in wallows, guns erupting in the night, legs of cloth and paper money powdered a dense fog through surfaces of silt for your foundation of the day.

BLINK

On the air beyond the house and in the house surrounding the men adhered around a single point—where light and air and sound had been before them the men's men knitted—the mother's flesh no longer crushed between. The bodies filled in around the house, warm pressure born in their want of light and knives and ice and ages and raw power and reform and trees and windows in dark summer in all our rising cities and the night above their heads and the night inside their colons and their past and future eggs and semen and their nipples and their cocks and wombs and private infestations and consolations—all they had and had not had held in the light there, contained in liquid, wrapped in skin.

The men burst men each from their seams, leaking others of them from the holes they carried. They caked their way upon the air. The woodwork around the house bowed and smoke, rutted with flesh from where they all wanted in at once. The splinters wedged into several skins, lifting their skin up, showing the coal black brunt of their disguising.

In the men's eyes were other eyes. In the eyes behind their eyes there were more eyes, fountains bursting liquid whips of water. The men were made of water that had once made up other men. Person 141 or Person 511 or Person 700,012 or Person 0, those before and those who'd never been. People of numbers without numbers or syllables in the bent strobe of their lungs, where as they struck upon the air they seemed no longer to remember they were there or ever had been or before already pressed forever in this moment in all hours pressed in the pages as the days' language changed around it.

Soon inside the house the force was so great that you could drop a thought and it would hover. You could speak your name and it would catch inside your throat and choke you as with rope and it still felt as waking up in a clean, familiar room. Every present instant stacked in calm uncolored prisms fused for miles en masse compressed in wordless urgeless milky moan.

The photographs of air the air was made of melted. The day gave darkness, a rind of black fitting the world.

BLINK

The men in light and men inside him in the room of the coil inside the house filled in around the space they called the child. They shot their bodies singing, and opened his mouth and looked between his teeth and gums for what was softest, for where they could feed on into the last. They searched the lids and lips and skin to show his hole after giving in his body or someone might hide something sweet. They shot his teeth and looked in along mites seeing moored in his craw. The son was gagging sounds. The walls of the gorge with ropes of saliva fragmented with hands covered every inch of him and through him all his family. His chest and shoulders blackened. With his eyes could see men. He could see everyone at once. In each man saw himself and many fathers—the injured father or father's eyes with broken glass and flowing pleated white beyond recognition—his father, the father remains under the other men in other years. The father had a lot of him, one for each mother hid in the mud around the house.

His hands were eddies in which men repeated, in which lines went where he began to bend—through the elongated body and through the many fathers. Numbers on their eyelids and his eyelids. His body leaned across the room into the room. The walls of the house began to loose convulsions. When all of him was empty, men filled his body with their old throes.

BLINK

BLINK

The father felt his flooding body. The presence stuttered through him and turned hard, baking veins flexed chalky soft. The sound of the men he could not see but was breathing in and out all through him made him stutter. He could not make his arms cease flailing. They no longer felt like his arms. He held the arms out before him and saw the meat sucking up in pills, becoming bulbous and rectangled. He turned the arms upended, elbows clicking where they touched. On the underarms he pushed his flab up— slick skin brushed with gravity and sound. Hid in his skin there was a blade there—a long metal gleaming ash. This was his mind. He licked his finger and slicked the blade to glisten, felt flashbulbs going off between his teeth and up his trachea. He turned to face the glowing.

BLINK

BLINK

BLINK

BLINK

BLINK

BLINK

If meat was not meat it was the word. Spirit of mold growth in heating wet spots in the form of working age and rising mist. Plates were illuminated walls inside the house, took a glowing refraction, and the legs and went and went. When anybody touched a body, where he crashed his older hum, rising slightly felt it slip into the rhythm of the lungs, the ring finger itching flesh, a blank page. It bled all through the holes in us, called veins. It was more serious than light. It knew the names of people. Think of them.

Between the lips, the lips were smiling, and then another, larger leaves, thick and shining down the shaft of day the house was. It had always been like this and would. The hour held the body around the neck of it and stretched it thicker in a glowing from the crevice of the gathered body of the hair, the chests, nipples and lacrimal glands, fingers, elbows, dimples and anus, navel—each through a hole in where the home was built there were leaves from the beginning—older bones. The bodies continued the cycle of low friction, lobes on each blade from the hot meat as the long hall of any being was forced to continue in his body in the flinch—in a strong and lustrous prismatic shape, adorned with every inhalation—the camera flashing, baked in size—begging for every minute.

BLINK

BLINK

BLINK

So, now late the father laughed. He felt as a force peeling, the cream that smelled every hour of your life. From the outside he looked like the same person as always, even less hair on his head, despite some version of the house of memory houses were all crammed in this decrepit body, where the sky founded its mend. What wormed itself upon the space and those among it was dry like paper and wide as light. In unpacked floods of fat beams old air moored upon each inch of the space from wall to wall. Though the endless glass setting the hall's size from the outside kept all itch of real glow from coming in—*whatever outside glow could be said to now remain*—the hum of fluorescent drafts set in the overhead bled reams of multi-plaid and blood red in long coils slit rapt shadow on the lengths and widths. The light, though white, or whatever other called can be called clear, the very air, had set compressed now with many colors: the color splinted through the rubber and came split—black as triple bruises, as unslept skin, as the inside of the body when the eyes are closed, making sentences that ran on and on, that both collapsed upon themselves and vast exploded in the midst of their creation, as a sentence should. Each time a body breathed in again what came into him there was less of him around him left to be, while beyond the disappearing something wider held him in.

BLINK

The child and then the father in the mother's house turned and found where where he'd felt the room there there were ten rooms, then there there were fifty, then then then fifty-thousand. Then came the colors, in reverse.

In the house around the mother the lights in the rooms blew open, each single bulb in slow procession split. With each the mother felt the light spreading on into her, wholly absorbed, her body rung with radiance and heat light. Inside her shape the mother found that she could both breathe and eat off of the liquid spurting there inside her and blurting from her body in the wash—she gave it off in bubbled grunts—liquid from her eyes and ears and nostrils, from her womb doors, from the condensed mesh of the many shrieking months she'd spent feeding food into herself to make more of her. Inside the liquid, further reams of film frames spooled in congregation. Her flesh had spread all through the room. It had no number. As well, the room had spread into the house, into the other rooms compacting, goggled with the eggs and all such what. As each room popped in convention with the tone, the mother felt the rooms appending to her—the house smeared and went on smearing, color for color in the wake of something warbling her body. The mother could not feel her systems. She could not feel her second self—the other presence having spread so wide and bulbous through and through her, it was now no longer there—it filled her lungs and slicked her back—it seeped among the walls into the house's air vents, its air and piping, the countless knobs and halls and wet—it laced among the house's wires, cracked the dust—it spread outside the house through hidden windows, coagulating in a cold wave over the ground—it washed thick over the spinning buildings, over the globulating earth, encombing trees hung gross with columned nits and colored sores bursting in the suspension with fat flowers and smeared up in the silver-gleaming jelly paste—over the crooked solar curtains and highest flight zones, annexed in field marks held in see-through lesions—among the weird glint of where the sun had sunk to lick the papered edge of the ex-sky burned and rubbled with stretchmarked brined designs of stuttered language—the waist on the skyhead pulling and panting, bored. In scream of beef and mutter pooling, the mother's liquid lapped the sun with her whole mind, and changed its color with vibrating, packed to black and neon burst in white, and in the color, too, the tone surrounding and surrounded, the sound of every door opened and then closed and clicking locked—then reopened to blue bodies—barfing nodules—to the sound of people sleeping in their threads, and side by side to other bodies beyond numbers, sweating off their names—the sound of one word spoken all together creamed with beeping along hallways with no walls and walls with nowhere in between them—the sound of white rinds stretching, rings on fingers sinking in—the sound of all things burst humming, all notes and nothing—the sound of all things folded over when. The sound was in the liquid and the liquid in the sound—the brim so fat it seemed any instant when the bath would wake in rupture, rise to squash upon the frying night.

BLINK

There was a massive clap then. There was the gonging. The house walls ran with juicing fluid, blooming bulbs as they rained down. The room was all around the mother bulging color. Her hips and lips and eyes had spread so wide she seemed a portal or filled with blank. There was a stink there swaddled on her washing. It called the birds into her brain. They burst from bejeweled cocooning patterns encrusted on the walls, the air, her flesh. Their wings were metal. No one. What. Their language flew in all at once together in one chirping endless chain head-on into her. When now. They stuffed their way on down inside her face, through her throat and belly and her ass, and from each point thereon outward, while at her cusp the air around the mother's liquid shone. Somewhere in the leak the leak was speaking. Its words weren't words but numbers, coiled in wads. Curds of syntax made in old names. The speech made the house's liquid cloudy. In the liquid there were eggs: one from each bird incubated and there laid into the mother's open bruises and her blood, such swelling bite marks of the laying written on her massive lungs and tongue and gums and glands and hair and gait and back and lard.

The colors screwed across the sky.

They screwed into the sky and through the sky and there before it.

The flesh from all holes fell.

It fell into the holes and through holes and held them.

Where there were no holes, more holes were made.

The holes were made until where all before there had been no holes there were the holes now, so that all holes forever were surrounded, like a feeling.

There were then no other words.

BLINK

The film was blinking.

BLINK

BLINK

The space was blinking.

BLINK

There was the sound.

There was the face.

The eye behind the face came open.

BLINK

BLINK

BLINK

BLINK

BLINK

BLINK

BLINK

Now it was everything, the eye.

Inside the house, the floor was inclined

The entry room was very long

Against the far wall, just slight out of reach, a small oblong shape sat cold

It was seated on a cube marked with a white plaque with white letters I could not read

The floors around the cube were very slick

They seemed to need to pull me to the center

A scrim of paper-colored water poured from beneath me where I touched the ground

I came near and touched the shape

I rubbed against the shape and rubbed it

The shape was any shape but here had one specific of which I cannot name the name

Where the shape touched on my skin its face made new over the new

Layers laying over old holes, bruises, smooth

I felt the air turn inside-out

All I wanted was for this to stop

I did not want to change again already

I could not sit the shape back down

In chrysalis the rooms made lotion

I threw up white

For many days I lived forever

I felt the door under my face

I could see many thousand other shapes inside the shape's face

Any shape at all

Inside the shapes someone was bleating my old language

I was not the child and not the father or the mother or the dark

I held the shape against my sternum

The celebration lights were gray

So much time passed and I'd done nothing

I hadn't even moved my arms

Through all the lives I'd felt cruise through me I was nowhere

It was snowing

Here the air was made of such light that it made the light already trundled on the air go curved

Slowing flexed out around the edges of my vision so that in this light here I saw the sky under the sky

It with our old names imprinted on it peeling

The sky wide with bodies hung from it in troves, fat pock-marked purses of slopping people

Colors not of how the skin had been in living, but the current state of their decay

Some of the bodies' globes glistened picked apart by gobs of sight and gnats grow fat off of the black-blistered ankles charred apart and caking pink

Among them, he who'd lived inside me for such stinging time and time regardless

Who'd therein eaten of my body and swaddled up a body of his own

Years in rooms where I could not see what he was doing, what he would make of what he had made of parts of us

Knowing without knowing

How I could hardly therein stand

The ages speaking loud inside my mind and bending over in my body

Ash of ash and ashes' ashes

The skin around my scalp and shoulders curling a crown out

Endless foreheads

Each punched in through warm and of no hold

You were one of those among it

Slathering in packets, skulls surrounding in the hour of my way

Sucking all my weight up through my body to my ideas

My heat, my limbs, my lust pulled into dust, days

All the scramming shit and mounds forever wedged in here now

In such strobing robes of light of we

And overhead the sky increasing, already having sucked its surface spotless

And underneath, the light-horizon, torched with tunnels of new smoke

Soft bodies blurting out a scrim of black so long and wide it could not be measured

Shit burst in replicate commotion spreading through and through the gone

Though my new eyes inside the eyes inside me

Older than water

Wider than all air

Opening the floor you'd carried in you hid forever

Floors into the day

In the room again I turned again to see what I had become

Inside the turning soon I tried to stop as I had started and could not stop

The day was spinning, so I was spinning

I found the room controlled by light

Spools were bursting from some center no longer included in the room's shape

The screen had quadrupled in its size

The film was blacker than my fever

The shape had disappeared

Or it had moved to some point in the room around me

The room just shook and shook

My spinning in the shaking at once made the other seem like calm

Like any day at all forever

I threw up gray

I threw up gold

Each time I said or thought or felt inside me the want for it to stop it went
on twice as fast and twice as hard

I threw up all the colors I remembered

All the colors of the Cone

I felt the colors all surround me

I got down on my knees

I went to squeeze the day against me in a warm way and found it no longer
at all there

No fold but just my arms now

I felt the air turn inside out again around me though in a different way than
just before

And in my acknowledgement of knowing it had done that it did exactly that again

And then again then and then again then

Increasing in its pace until I could no longer tell when it had happened

What was becoming

Under great sun, without number

We were so large now in the house now

The houses there surrounding all surrendered and made cold

We were liquid, snug with vision, so much of all that someone stitching
into me, stitched

We in the day had such dimension

The rooms drawn cold and clinging to my face

In each room there was and would be someone

The man, the men, the child, me, you

Each of us a body

Each in skin

All of it thinning by the hour, in the house, our whole

Each room around our mush went on for our whole lives each

The mold grew quickly, barking color, prism panes

There were gardens

I was young then, I had a burnt mind and clean lungs, I had a body

All of we did

All of we never have

There was wire

The weeks controlled themselves and passed in ash

The years were greasing

The house all bloated and the choirs in our eyes

The girth of burnt flesh in the hardened ocean

The liquidated sun

The way the ground had lurched to smack the sky

To mash against our groaning bodies, squeeze us leaking out the sides

All bent in black above our format

Billions

Edges

Ages

Around each sound the world went on

This had happened many times before and would and would and would
again

Floors and floors of doors for years held up above us and below with our
skin folding into cities, waiting

Unto no threshold

I'd asked you not to come this far

I asked you suncloaked in the blanking

Those turned up backwards in the smear

Those who I would recognize even dismantled, bring them to me

Bring me those who I would not

Each of us another day for us beginning

Please, as this light is too much light for any hour with our name writ in the crease

You there folding under no night, or laying silent, or walking low on along a longer wall

Now you are in here

Now you must watch our shape revolve

You cannot see the shape but you can be it

It is your body in your sleep

It is the blood in your cerebrum

It has been always

Nights now this house is very still

The walls are walls and air is walls and you are walls and I am walls

There are the birds

Their eggs lain in our folding

When I move my mouth I hear them hulk

I hear the words they must surrender

I hear them spit up in their babies' mouths, into yours

The words

They cream and cream inside my mind for hours

This long evening

Any evening

A song comes out but there's no sound

What hold had come for us again, what years of frying nothing in clasp of corridors encombed, the blue long buildings in a prism captured and ingested and choked upon and bent and shat into the light to writhe again among the manner of a person, a brimming body with out lungs and load of veins milked without waking, it would not bend, it would not cease, inside the mounds I walked for hours even unnamed and was still right there with all the towers underground in tones all ending and beginning in such succession I could no longer recall having heard any single one of them alone at all and had always been only on in endless drift of furor, there had never been a wall, no edge of leg of lymph between me and my mind or child or range of age, the Cone had pulled us all apart again only for pleasure, a ream of bees flexed from our squat, the machines we had imagined in depression to have beings to have bodies to have glow, a tired light that filled the houses while all through all air the words went on and books turned open and emphatic spraying ink into the ink, any word forever having changed unnumbered times up till the instant of our seeing and looking down and framing in, syllables in their eternal damage milked and quilted through what linings any hour could contain while through the halls our skins changed textures and changed tone and did not move and the digits flashed all through our eyes where we were hungry or were horny or were blown, the child inside the child again all screaming disease eating money humping torrents watching serpents controlling nothing in the tone's light in the Cone's name come down again to clasp against the blank we'd always aimed and build edges and build rooms there and resound while for each inch there were a thousand faces and for each face a thousand eyes and in each eye a thousand colors and in each color every sound and in each sound all of the words already named and unremembered where in each memory a lock, locks laid in doors and doors unending through the milk there into corridors we called our flesh of lard so large we could not shave it in the hour of the sun and so again must split again and live it and begin it and need more and never have enough in any instance to be silent and eat the magnet and live where we had already been before

I knew my child needed to need me, I knew I needed it to need and to know I knew that it had though would not always, this was the vast unending thread, this was the cord that killed my lungs each hour pressed against the houses that I knew and walked me through the beaches and the armies as I had lived them in my mind for what I'd been, there was no color I could not look in and see me stammered in there ripped apart beaten already by the machines where before I rose an arm or eye inside this light, I knew and knew and yet at no point could I be stopped, not at any aim of waver in the going I would go through would I be ended till I did, this was the vast condition of my organism, beyond the

dreamspeech and the pill, beyond the black collaboration forced upon me until I
was stopped I could not be stopped, I would go forward in the meld and make of
this beyond all surface before the surface tore me up, each hour held me in it and
was the hour and was passed, come what way would kill in any coming minute
there had already been such prior light, the cities could be crushed by any of us
every of us every way again began and yet in the seam the singe was written all
requiring no words, no book that could be erased or cold or fonted, no gold script
on sanded leaf, black castles in a flat mirror, purple fortunes, and so must be
for any rind, any eye stitched in the smallest lungs from the beginning, beyond
the verb, and so among the prisms there was no fortress and nothing clawing
beyond length and no moon above laughed for whoever to come reigning night
in us again, say what you will but I was opened, had been conditioned, knew
the stone, could kiss the stone inside my mind without permission and what
beyond it I could turn to anything again my own, stuffed beyond however many
of me held and wondered, every private inch to have again, to rub again and
not remember if I did not wish

And so where the Cone had owned me I was ancient and I was anybody's guess,
what colors crashed could crash forever and both begin and end my face, though
on beyond the face there was the field there and the field was spinning and the
water shook inside my lungs and sound adhered to nothing and did not speak
and all directions were the same and all names laughed thick hard ceilings bent
beneath us and the fire and the mass, we burned through film and gear and
mechanism, though idea and charm and make, the buttons pressed themselves
and cursed themselves where they were wanted and the ash rained from the night
and the dark turned over and showed where forever it'd been rubbed, bright

knives of catalogs and barking pillared in silence spent for something old to do,
walls erected and dismantled and erected and dismantled and erected along the
lines barfed in the seas the hour flung against the walls inside the Cone to petrify
us, and so it did, and in our linings even unlined the colors burnt themselves
and rose again, caulking in each bright uprising brutal prisms where the colors
in their hue had always hid, beaten dark upon the day now where no day was to
skull along the edges of what anyone had been, the pixels rising, the seas inside
them punctured, rolled raw like axes in a snarl, the older sound of someone
waking up beside you in the darkness gifted again where no light had ever been
to call the urge, crashed where crashing could not happen, grown new cold ovens
in a rip where for every instant the day was rising and now could open up its
sizeless mouth and breathe us in, another throat inside the skin there, light
vibrating, chords hammered under chords, an egg for every apple, a summer
sprawling in a domed hole, where by this now we could climb

The ice of higher folds was brighter and held us closer and chewed our shapes,
it bent around us and began us and ripped through the seam of any page and
any inch of what a house was or how many and the linings of the word crapped
and tottered in our centers already growing, it licked the bubbles from the ash, it
turned the keyboard over and typed the flat side until the frame broke and in the
center there was flesh, it kissed the flesh and all its wires in splitting systems while
we held inside it still and watched, each old letter lapped into us as centuries
of rain and rolling planets, we closed what eyes we had remaining, we closed
behind those eyes and eyes behind those until there was no visible retort and at
last the field now could be centered and in the colors we could see no phrase of
blinking or bright desire beyond the instant of us would now begin, no menu

in the choir, no shrieking digit, where in the frame each inch of film had prior passed the wanting left to lay and lurk over one another in blessed dementia so that all the black was all the way, there knew no gesture to the definition now required, there were no hallways and no floors, no box to open or cells to splinter in our body to persist, we did not have to wait to be restarted, we did not have to wonder to be washed, who and who the who was held no question and the ice of all our ice was not in pain

No layer here was destined nor not destined, no layer here had not been lost, the cold worked inside the cold and flayed it outwards though not extending as there was no space beyond the way, no phrase beyond the softing though in the water of it we could walk and could go on in any way we wanted and have been so, any day could seem the next, I might look down and find my arms there typing language and believe the language and know it was or I would look down and find the words there in my body written always, I could hold my body as a book, I could put the book down and walk into the next room and see the walls there and touch the walls and hold their sound, the sun above the fields would rise and fall like any way of us had ever, I could touch and be touched, hold and be held, could speak and be spoke into, could spread the word all through my blood, where any shape here appeared it always listened and when I turned it turned around, each line inside the field forever shifting in my vision as I needed without knowing that I did, each old color in the presence of its colors, waking, slaying, being, in the warm name of any coming memory of skin

Each new fold became again folded newly as they folded where each shape coursed for my veins and eyes and wandered fat, it shook around it what was mentioned, it gave me children and gave cities, it gave me diseases and great panic, it gave me a soil in which to lie, the same such soil in which could be placed any other of me that I needed to be held there beyond my body while shape and sound would work it down, you would call it years but it had been years already and already once again, it is okay, where we would walk the days would let us, the walls would not fold beyond our time, though what our time was in this feeling could not seem endless until it had ended and we were taken by the hand, this was the gift and the decision, it had always been agreed, our name in the white books in the white ink arousing fires for the purpose of a dark, a shape of any shape suspended in a glowing before around the edges it must burn and become ours

Yes we were loved, no there was no specific reason or body who could love us, yes the days surrounded us beyond our need though they were not days, yes we might have liked to stay inside the house inside the hour aching spindled in a rash, the persons in persons piling in us until there seemed so many the color came upon us on our own, yes the light would size around us like all the clothes we'd ever breathed inside of or against, each sound funneled through and through the sound surrounding aboveground, like all the humming through the beings, for every inch where we'd been brushed and every instant we'd been flooded, every wallow of the ash, we could can hold the word inside our shape inside the evening for as long as we would like unwound, and the light will hold us and the shape will hold us up

The time between the tone goes on the prayer goes on the flesh goes on the day goes on the want goes on in all this folding the milk goes on the soil goes on the thrush goes on the bark goes on the gold goes on the tone goes on, there is the day, it is any day for all of us again where we have folded and must fold and so again, you don't have to raise a flesh you don't have to turn a page and yet you will or you will not and for all of this I become you and we become you and the word is in your lungs, you cannot breathe the word

The rooms in here where we have centered and the hue around our having, the split of skin where all have entered and the crush of sound commands a sound split from which there has never been a silence and never would be, itch for itch and light for eye, node for pink inside the insect of what incoming as it exits from its sleeve in dreamless meat where no one sleeps, a cream inside a cord, a lung inside a slowing, each day shaved beyond its prior phrasing's aping woke

Where what had been forgiven is what must be forgiven, what had been forgotten must be lost, cold long char of brain meat crushed between two words until the field is flatter than the rind inside a floe burst from bursting uncommanded before the mouth could open wide enough to give the body air, the cells aflutter, the dust aflutter, where to flutter is to want

The grain in the game of the soft of the nape of the wet of the gray of the back of the scape of the showering conundrum pricking open and surrounded and surrounding all absorbed all cracked agate in the earthless furnace tongued with expectation

Waved to spark the seizing through its surface past the stirrup and the phase, what could have stung itself in pleasure lifting the lids on what had held

So long carried on in bulk repeating the shape began to look exactly like itself

All hours pressed in any instant

Now

Blake Butler lives in Atlanta.

Thanks to Dawn Raffel of *The Literarian* & David McClendon of *Unsaid Magazine*, where portions of *Sky Saw* previously appeared.

Other Works by Blake Butler:
Ever
Scorch Atlas
There Is No Year
Nothing: A Portrait of Insomnia
Anatomy Courses (with Sean Kilpatrick)